W9-BZP-701

◯ THE
CLEAR
MOMENT

Ed McClanahan

THE CLEAR MOMENT

COUNTERPOINT BERKELEY

Some of these stories appeared in *Ace Weekly*, *Open 24 Hours*, *Kentucky Monthly*, and *Louisville Magazine*. "Great Moments in Sports" and "Another Great Moment in Sports" originally appeared in *My Vita, If You Will* (Counterpoint, 1998). Portions of "And Then I Wrote . . ." originally appeared in *Famous People I Have Known* (Farrar, Straus & Giroux, 1985). "Fondelle" was published in 2002 in a hand-set, letterpress edition by Larkspur Press of Monterey, Kentucky. "A Foreign Correspondence" was published in 2002 as a limited-edition chapbook by Sylph Publications in Tucson, Arizona. A shorter version of "The Imp of Writing" was published as a broadside by Ken Sanders Rare Books/Dreamgarden Press (Salt Lake City, Utah) in 2005.

Library of Congress Cataloging-in-Publication Data

McClanahan, Ed.
O the clear moment / Ed McClanahan.
p. cm.
ISBN-13: 978-1-58243-430-8
ISBN-10: 1-58243-430-1
1. Autobiographical fiction, American. I. Title
PS3563.C339708 2008
813'.54—dc22   2008012039

Front cover design by Ralph Steadman
Interior design by David Bullen
Printed in the United States of America

COUNTERPOINT
2117 Fourth Street
Suite D
Berkeley, CA 94710
www.counterpointpress.com

Distributed by Publishers Group West

10   9   8   7   6   5   4   3   2   1

for Tom and Brenda Marksbury

for Kent Crockett

for Joe Petro III

for Johnny Lackey

for Merce and Heidi and Hugo, our three angels

—and especially for Shelley Christine Morss,

   my very first true heartthrob,

and Baby Jessie, my very latest

Contents

THE CLEAR MOMENT

GREAT MOMENTS IN SPORTS

O the clear moment, when from the mouth
A word flies, current immediately
Among friends; or when a loving gift astounds
As the identical wish nearest the heart;
Or when a stone, volleyed in sudden danger,
Strikes the rabid beast full on the snout!
    Robert Graves, "Fragment of a Lost Poem"

Like everybody else, I've told my favorite sports stories so many times I almost believe them myself. For instance:

When I was twelve years old (stop me if you've heard this), Happy Chandler gave me an autographed baseball. I once rode on an elevator with Jim Thorpe. I know a guy who knows a guy whose father once stood next to Lou Gehrig at a urinal in Yankee Stadium. I saw Ewell "The Whip" Blackwell pitch a no-hitter for the Cincinnati Reds in 1947, and Tom Seaver duplicate the feat in the next Reds game I attended—thirty-one years later. Gay Brewer, Jr., the golfer, once bird-dogged my girlfriend. My friend Gurney Norman claims to have tossed a Ping-Pong ball into a Dixie cup from twenty feet away. (I believe him, of course—but hey, what are friends for?) Waite Hoyt once let my uncle buy him a drink. In college, I was employed as a "tutor" by my university's athletic department, in which capacity I took, by correspondence, an entire sophomore English literature survey course for a first-string All-American tackle.

("Now don't get me no A," my protégé cautioned, the night before I was to take the final for him. "Get me about a C+, that'd be about right." It was a line I would put to use twenty-five years later in my one and only novel, *The Natural Man*, still available at fine booksellers everywhere.)

Well, I could go on, but modesty forefends; my record in Vicarious Athletics speaks for itself.

Yet there were a few times when I actually got into the fray in person, in the quest after that elusive Perfect Moment. Like the time I ran fourteen balls in a game of straight pool (and had a straight-in shot at the fifteen—and scratched). Or the time I won a dollar and thirty-five cents in half an hour pitching pennies on the courthouse steps (and lost it all back in the next twenty minutes).

Or the time twelve guys on our high school basketball

team came down with the flu, and I was abruptly—not to say precipitously—elevated from second-string JV to the furthermost end of the varsity bench, and suddenly found myself, deep in the third quarter, not only in the game but also endeavoring to guard the great Cliff Hagan, then of Owensboro High, later of the University of Kentucky Wildcats and the St. Louis Hawks. On the first play he broke for the basket and went twinkle-toeing up my chest like he was Fred Astaire and I was the Stairway to the Stars.

Hagan—Mr. Hagan—accumulated eleven points during my two-minute tenure, mostly on shots launched from some vantage point afforded him by my reclining anatomy. If there were a statistic called "percentage of defensive assists," I'd have set some kind of record.

Still, every mutt has his Moment, and mine was coming up.

By the spring of 1950, when I was a junior at Maysville High and my glory days on the hardwood were but a distant memory ("Mac," our estimable Coach Jones had said, drawing me aside one day after practice, "Mac, you're a good, hardworking boy, but son, your hands are small, and I just don't believe you've got the equipment to make this team"), I had long since limited my athletic exertions to the rigorous pursuit of female companionship.

In other words, I was spending a disproportionate amount of time mooning about the house and grounds of a certain Mr. and Mrs. T. C. Stonebreaker, who had four beautiful daughters still at home. Alas, I was but one of many, a restive, milling herd of rampant teenage billy goats strutting our dubious stuff before the less-than-awestruck Misses Stonebreaker. On Saturday afternoons (when Mr. Stonebreaker usually beat a strategic withdrawal to his euchre game at the Moose Lodge, while Mrs. Stonebreaker did her grocery shopping), the testosterone level in Stonebreaker Hall could have peeled the wallpaper.

For these occasions, we trotted out all our highly developed social skills—which is to say we maligned and demeaned and bullied and belittled one another mercilessly, in the hope of raising our own stature in the eyes of the four (largely indifferent) fascinators; we cut up and showed off like drunken sailors, and talked as indelicately as we dared, for the edification of that beguiling audience.

Such was the scenario on that memorable Saturday afternoon in the spring of 1950, the day of my Personal Best Great Moment:

Mr. S. is at his euchre, Mrs. S. is out shopping, and the house fairly teems with postpubescent boys of every size and description, from eighth-graders vying for the attentions of Gracie, the youngest Stonebreaker, to a couple of pipe-puffing college freshmen home for the weekend expressly to pay court to Mary Margaret, the eldest, who graduated from high school last year and now has an office job at the cotton mill. Once again, the objects of our affection have reduced us all—even the college guys—to the developmental level of the eighth-graders, who themselves are behaving like fifth-graders. Naturally, there have already transpired numerous episodes of pantsing, not to mention various hotfoots, noogies, and wedgies; and the atmosphere is redolent of bathroom humor so sophisticated it has left the sisters Stonebreaker fairly gasping with (let us hope) admiration.

I'm there too, of course, but for once I've held myself aloof from these adolescent proceedings, having somehow cornered Bernice, who is to my mind the fairest Stonebreaker of them all, over by the piano, where I and my Lucky Strike are demonstrating my prowess at French inhaling, blowing smoke rings, and—like Tony Curtis on the cover of the paperback of *The Amboy Dukes* ("A Novel of Wayward Youth in Brooklyn! Now a Thrilling Motion Picture!")—making suave conversation while the Lucky is parked roguishly in the corner of my mouth. I have also lately cultivated, in the wake of my departure from the uniformly crew-cut Bulldog squad, a prodigious Wildroot-lubricated pompadour, complete with a lank Tony Curtis forelock that dangles ornamentally over my right eye, and I'm sporting my brand-new oh-so-cool two-tone jacket with the collar turned up—just like Tony's!

("How come you've got your collar turned up that way, Eddie?" Bernice has just interrupted my suave conversation to inquire. "It's not a bit cold in here!")

And now into this tranquil domestic circle swagger the last two guys in all of Christendom whom the rest of us—the

males, I mean—want to see, namely the dread Speedy Little
Guards (so-called in the local press), a brace of Bobbys—
let's call them Bobby One and Bobby Two—indispensable
Bulldog mainstays, One a razzle-dazzle ball handler, Two a
nonpareil set-shot artist, both of them brash, bandy-legged,
and, in the unanimous opinion of the Stonebreaker girls,
devastatingly cute.

Bernice quickly escapes the narrow confines of our tête-à-
tête and joins her sisters, who are gathered round the Bobbys
to admire their new Bulldog letter sweaters, acquired just
last night at the annual awards banquet. (How come they're
wearing sweaters? I hear myself grumbling inwardly. It's not
a bit cold in here!) Then we all troop dutifully outside to see
Bobby Two's new short—actually his mother's new short, a
dumpy, frumpy 1950 Nash Rambler whose contours, come
to think of it, are not unlike those of Mrs. Two herself.

Still, the Nash is profoundly snazzier than the scuffed
penny loafers which at present constitute my own principal
means of locomotion, and I am positively viridescent with
envy. And this condition is further aggravated by my growing
certainty that if Bobby Two has his way, he and Bernice will
be snuggling up in that goddamn Rambler at the RiverView
Drive-in Theater tonight.

Once we're all back inside the house, the two Bobbys,
along with Marcella, the second-eldest sister, and (sigh)
Bernice, promptly disappear into the kitchen, from whence
soon begin to issue various muffled giggles, sniggers, chortles,

titters, and similar sounds of suppressed merriment. Meanwhile, the eighth-graders are entertaining Gracie with a tiny-tuba ensemble of rude armpit noises as the pipe-puffers regale Mary Margaret with BMOC tales (featuring, of course, themselves), leaving the rest of us Lotharios to loll about the living room shooting pocket pool while we feign indifference to the jolly goings-on behind the kitchen door.

After ten or fifteen minutes the merrymakers emerge, the girls still all a-giggle behind their hands, the Bobbys all a-smirk. Each Bobby is carrying, inexplicably, an egg.

"Okay," Bobby One announces, stepping to the center of the room, "now let's see which one can bust his egg on the othern's head!" With that, he and Bobby Two begin comically bouncing around the room on their toes like sparring spermweights until, after a brief and thoroughly unpersuasive flurry of pseudo-fisticuffs, Bobby One, egg in hand, smacks Bobby Two on the noggin and—how could I have been so surprised by this?—mirabile dictu, the egg's not loaded, there's nothing in it. The empty shell shatters harmlessly on Bobby Two's crew-cut pate.

Of course the Bobbys—being Bobbys—act like this is the greatest joke since the chicken crossed the road. There wasn't nothing to it, they aver, clapping each other on the back in the throes of their hilarity; we just punched little pinholes in them eggs and blowed the insides out.

And right there is where I make the dumbest move of my young life.

"Let's see that one," I hear myself saying, unaccountably, to Bobby Two, whose egg—whose eggshell—is still intact. "Lemme take a look at it." To this day, I don't know what in the world I was thinking of.

"You wanna see the egg?" says Bobby One. "Hey Bob-o, Clammerham wants to see the egg!"

Bobby Two is grinning, and there is a gleam in his eye that should have given me pause. Could that be a corresponding gleam in the eye of Bernice, who is standing just behind him? Why do I feel like I'm in a play, and everybody knows the script but me?

"Sure, Hammerclam," says Bobby Two, putting his hands behind his back. "Which hand?"

Christ, I'm thinking, it's only an eggshell. But hey, I got my forelock, got my Lucky hangin' on my lip, I'm cool. So I play along.

"Uh, the left?"

"Nope," he says, showing me his left hand, in which there is, of course, nothing at all. Meanwhile his right hand—in which there is, of course, not an eggshell but an egg, in all its fullness—is describing a high, sweeping arc from behind his back to the top of my head, where it arrives with a disgusting splat, much to the disadvantage of my pompadour.

"Sorry," says Bobby Two, wiping his palm on my Tony Curtis lapel, "wrong hand."

So there I stand in the Stonebreaker living room with a coiffure nicely dressed out in egg yolk, a viscous thread of egg white trailing, like a sneeze gone terribly wrong, from my forelock to my Lucky Strike, and all about me a tumult of eighth-graders rolling on the floor, college boys roaring, Stonebreaker girls hugging themselves in their mirth, Bobbys pounding each other on the back to the point of bodily injury. My dignity, I fear, has been seriously compromised. Time to regroup.

To which purpose I slink off to the kitchen, where I stick my sodden head under the faucet in the sink and shampoo my hair as best I can with dishwashing liquid, dry it with Mrs. Stonebreaker's dishtowel, and sponge off my jacket with her dishrag. Then I comb my hair; the egg yolk residue is beginning to set up, which actually helps a little in the reconstruction of my pompadour. Finally, I go to the refrigerator and help myself to two more of Mrs. Stonebreaker's eggs. Thus armed, I return to the scene of Clamhammer's Humiliation.

In the living room, things have sorted themselves out predictably, in accordance with the New Social Order: The armpit ensemble has resumed serenading Gracie, and the college stuffed shirts, solemn as owls, are once again puffing industriously away on their calabashes, throwing up a smoke screen around Mary Margaret as dense—and certainly as aromatic—as an enchantment. But now Bobby One is cozying up to Marcella on the sofa, and Bernice, that Jezebel, has joined Bobby Two over by the piano—in *our* corner!

Such is the sordid scene that Clamhammer the Redeemer

bursts upon, with blood in his eye and vengeance on his mind.

"Awright, you sorry bastids," I thunder—yes! I actually thundered!—brandishing an egg at first one Bobby, then the other, "now I would hate to have to throw this right here in Mrs. Stonebreaker's living room, but I've got one of these apiece for you two sonsabitches, and if you're not outta here by the time I count to three, you're definitely gonna get egged! One!"

The Bobbys exchange stricken glances, and I know that I am terrible in my wrath.

"Two!"

Now Bobby One half-rises from the sofa, while the craven Bobby Two endeavors to shield himself behind Bernice.

"Three!" I cry, and with that the Bobbys break simultaneously for the doorway into the front hall, and I am in hot pursuit, my throwing arm cocked at the ready. But not for nothing do their admirers call them the Speedy Little Guards, for by the time I make the hall, they are scrambling out the front door. And the truth is that, despite my threat, I am not quite willing to throw an egg within these sacred premises, owing to the certainty that Mrs. Stonebreaker would forthwith banish me from the temple forever and ever, world without end.

So I hold my fire, and in another instant I'm on the front stoop and the Bobbys are already legging it across the street toward where the Rambler awaits them. I reach the curb just as Bobby Two arrives at the Rambler's driver's-side door, and I have a clear shot at him, a perfect target inasmuch as, even if I miss, I'll still hit his mommy's car. Then, just as I'm going into my windup, what suddenly looms up between us but a city bus, lumbering along as huge and pokey as a steamship. And when the bus is out of the way at last, I see that Bobby Two is at the Rambler's wheel, revving up, and his door is closed. Bobby One is just opening the passenger-side door; I can see his head above the roof of the car, so I uncork a desperation throw at it, not a bad throw, actually, except that he sees it coming and ducks into the car as the egg sails over his head and splatters abortively against a telephone pole. Then Bobby Two pops the clutch, and the Rambler scratches off more spiritedly than I would've dreamed it could, while I stand there on the curb shaking my fist after them, a masterful study in futility.

But wait, what's this I see! Down at the far end of the block, the Rambler is hanging a U-ey! Can it be that they're actually going to come back past me? Yes they are; the Rambler has wallowed through its turn, and is headed back in my direction. Maybe they've forgotten that I still have an egg in my arsenal—and this time, I am vowing grimly as I palm my egg, I won't miss.

As the Rambler rolls slowly past, Bobby One has his thumbs in his ears, and is making donkey faces at me behind the passenger-side window. I draw a bead on his ugly mug and cut loose a vicious Ewell "The Whip" Blackwell sidearm bullet that I know even as it leaves my hand is a wild pitch, and that it will miss the strike zone by half a yard.

Now there are those who will maintain that an egg is, after all, only an egg, a stupid, insensate, ovoid article of no cognitive power whatsoever unless and until it somehow gets a chicken in it—itself a species not conspicuous for its intellect. But that does not describe *this* egg. For this is *my* egg, friends, as surely as if I'd laid it myself, and this egg is smarter, even, than its proud parent; it has a mind of its own and knows *exactly* where it wants to go. And this egg of mine has *eyes*, dear hearts, and as it spins off my fingertips it sees what I have not seen, which is that although Bobby One has his window snugly closed, his wind-wing—that little triangular vent that all cars used to have, back in the days when carmakers were smarter than, say, chickens—his wind-wing is . . . wide open!

And this little egg of mine *finds* that tiny opening with all its eyes, and it flies as true as Cupid's arrow straight through the vent and explodes in a bright golden sunburst all *over* the interior of Bobby Two's mommy's brand new short, all *over* those accursed Bobbys and their goddamn letter sweaters! Thus have I struck the rabid beast full on the snout!

Luck? You dare call it luck? Was it luck that directed Gurney's Ping-Pong ball into that Dixie cup? No indeed. Luck, I think, is synonymous with money; it's strictly a business proposition, wherein good luck produces a payoff, bad luck a payout. Nor, of course, was it skill; neither I nor

Gurney could duplicate our feats in a thousand thousand years. No, this was destiny, pure and simple; we had, each of us, a blind date with Immortality. Did Cliff Hagan ever toss a Ping-Pong ball into a Dixie cup at twenty feet? Did Ewell the Whip ever fling an egg through the wind-wing of a moving car?

And while I'm asking questions, I'll ask these: Were the Stonebreaker girls all watching from the stoop when my egg burst like a de Kooning masterpiece inside the Rambler? Did they scream and squeal like bobby-soxers when this miracle of art and magic and athletic prowess transpired right before their very eyes? Did Bernice and I go to the movies that night—the sit-down movies, not the drive-in— and did I, when I took her home afterward, kiss her on the lips on that very stoop?

No, sports fans, I'm afraid not, I'm afraid not. But . . . O the clear moment!

HEY SHOOBIE!

A few years ago, someone asked me to contribute to a book about the classic Southern funeral, and especially about the tradition of comforting the bereaved with a bountiful spread of down-home comestibles. The book hasn't happened yet, but the request reminded me that I've instructed my friends to throw a going-away party for me when I check out, and that I'm confident they'll see to it that there are plenty of good eats on hand and, knowing my friends, plenty to wash 'em down with. My favorite "final arrangement," though, has to do not with the grub and grog (excellent though I know they'll be) but with that most indigestible of articles, my tombstone.

When I was a tyke growing up in the late 1930s in Brooksville, Kentucky—which as everybody knows is the capital of commerce and culture of all of Bracken County—my dearest pal was a kid named James Hubert Hamilton, whose double-barreled given names I conflated (say them aloud, and you'll see why) into the monicker "Shoobie." He's long since been known to *tout le monde* as "Jim," but for seventy years now, I alone have persisted in calling him Shoobie, just as he's the last man standing who still dares to call me by my old Brooksville name, which is, I blush to say, "Sonny."

Shoobie and I lived on Church Street, only about half a block apart, and we played together all day long when school was out. It was our boyish ritual that whichever of us was released first from the breakfast table would run out into the placid street and holler, at the top of his piping little voice, "Hey Shoo-o-o-o-bie!" or "Hey Son-n-n-n-ny!" Thus began our days of frolic and leisure, mischief and delight.

Brooksville—"population seven hundred when they're all at home," as the citizenry liked (and perhaps still does) to characterize itself—was an ideal, idyllic place to be a child in, a tiny little island of a country town with half a dozen stores that stocked, among them, an endless array of all the fundamental necessities of life—candy bars and chewing gum and rat cheese and baloney sandwiches and soda pop and comic books and Popsicles—and a palatial courthouse at the epicenter of it all, and Shoobie and I had the run of the whole metropolitan complex, all day long, every day.

From the age of five or six, we knew each and every one of those seven hundred citizens as well as they knew us, and we could go, for all practical purposes, anywhere we wanted— and in those days we wanted to go . . . everywhere!

Together, we prowled the courthouse all the way from the basement to the clock tower that topped it off, and sledded madly on Church Street Hill, and snooped on couples smooching in their cars out by the county rock crusher, and, in the heat of summer, pursued the horse-drawn ice wagon through the streets of Brooksville begging for chips of ice, or carried cane fishing poles on our shoulders to the reservoir like little escapees from the cover of the *Saturday Evening Post*. Together, as we grew older and our pleasures grew more daring and sophisticated, we climbed to the top of the water tower—a hundred breathtaking feet straight up, a hundred rungs on the steel ladder!—and tested the heady joys of tobacco. When we were thirteen or fourteen, Shoobie got the coolest job of all time, as popcorn popper and ticket catcher at the New Lyric Theatre—but whenever he came down with chicken pox or mumps or some other inconvenient affliction, I was his backup.

(Those happy few who are acquainted with my afore-mentioned novel, *The Natural Man*, may recall the New Artistic Theatre, where Harry Eastep had Shoobie's job. And I suppose this is as opportune a time as any to warn the tenderhearted that I intend to flog that poor old novel unmercifully in the ensuing pages.)

Mr. Bales (Mr. Ockerman in the novel), who owned the theater, also ran the Brooksville roller rink, and Shoob and I both worked there too, putting clamp-on skates on other kids, for tips. This being small-town Kentucky in the post-war 1940s, it will come as no surprise that we weren't exactly raking in the dough; but skate-boys got to skate for free, so for a while there we spent more time on our wheels than on our feet, and soon we were—at least in our own estimation— the two best skaters in Bracken County. One Saturday after-noon, a new girl turned up at the rink, and Shoobie and I nearly broke our respective necks showing off for her. The new arrival, Joyce, evidently found Shoobie's moves more edifying than mine, for they quickly became sweethearts, and today, sixty years later, they still are.

In 1948, at the end of my fifteenth summer, my folks and I moved to Maysville, twenty miles east. I had acquired a Bracken County sweetie of my own by then, so I imagined I'd be bouncing back to Brooksville like a bad penny—after all, what's twenty miles to a man in love with Patty Ann Redden?—but, in fact, it didn't quite work out that way. Maysville (population seven *thousand* when they're all at home!) was the Moulin Rouge compared to Brooksville's Podunk (Excuse me, beloved, but that's how it seemed in 1948), and it developed that Patty Ann and I apparently weren't soul mates after all, for, unlike Shoobie and Joyce, she and I forsook one another almost instantly after I moved away, and to my recollection we never laid eyes on each other ever again.

But Shoobie and I did share one more quite memorable occasion—although, for reasons that will shortly become apparent, the word "memorable" may be ill-chosen, for there is much of the occasion that I can't recall at all. At any rate, this much I am sure of:

Just one month after my family's move to Maysville, I spent the weekend of my sixteenth birthday back in Brooksville, visiting Shoobie. On Saturday night, he and I put together four bucks and gave it to John Burton, the town's most notorious—and certainly its most malodorous—drunk, to buy two pints of Sneaky Pete (for the uninitiated, which we certainly were, Sneaky Pete is a nickname for extremely cheap and exceptionally nasty sweet red wine), one pint for the preternaturally fragrant Mr. Burton, one for Shoob and me. Like many households in Brooksville in those days, the Hamiltons didn't have indoor plumbing, so Shoob and I took our pint to the outhouse, where we glugged it down and, swacked to the gills for the first time in our young lives, dropped the empty bottle down the hole, into . . . archaeology.

Nowadays Shoobie and I live about seventy-five miles apart—he and Joyce in northern Kentucky, I and my wife, Hilda, in Lexington—which ain't exactly hollerin' distance, so we don't communicate quite as regularly as we did in the days of our ladhood. But we do stay in touch, mostly by way of lengthy phone calls once or twice a year. And one night five or six years ago, he called to tell me that he and Joyce had driven down to Brooksville recently to choose their burial plot in the pretty little cemetery there.

As it happens, many members of my own family rest, presumably in peace, in that same cemetery, and it had long been my intention to request that when I buy the farm, the Brooksville Cemetery is where it will be located. Indeed, by the most remarkable coincidence, on the night Shoobie called, I was in the very act of writing a letter regarding my funeral instructions to my attorney, Bob Z., with whom I had an appointment in the next few days for a discussion of my will.

"I prefer," I had already written, "to be cremated, in the most efficient, least expensive, least ostentatious manner available. (I did live fast and love hard, but I didn't manage to die young; therefore I won't leave a handsome corpse, so there's no need to put it on display.) I have no objection to a memorial occasion whereat everybody testifies as to what a splendid fellow I used to be (the Mormon Tabernacle Choir would be a nice addition), as long as my mourners observe these solemnities in the course of a party good enough to make me wish I'd been invited to it."

I had requested too, in the letter, that my burial plot be marked by a modest headstone—and late that night, after Shoobie's call, I added this:

"It would also give me great posthumous pleasure if the words 'Hey Shoobie!' could be inscribed, in small, discreet letters, on the back of the stone. And please don't forget the exclamation point!"

FONDELLE or, THE WHORE WITH A HEART OF GOLD

But I was one-and-twenty,
No use to talk to me.
    A. E. Housman

In 1954, the summer before my senior year in college (at Miami University—the one in Ohio, alas), my dad, a small-time Maysville, Kentucky, businessman with pretty good contacts among the lower political life forms that grace our benighted state, somehow gathered up all his chits at once and used them to prevail upon our congressman, one Rep. Bates, to arrange a summertime job for me on a road crew in Yosemite National Park, at the other end of the world in California. Although I'd gone to Europe on a student tour the previous summer, this would be, literally, the first time I'd been west of Paducah.

What a summer! I lived in a tent-cabin (a tent with a wooden frame and floor) beneath the great Ponderosa pines and Douglas firs of Yosemite Valley, within sight of the majesty of El Capitan and within earshot of the roar of Bridalveil Falls. I earned the amazing sum of two-seventy-five an hour—that would've covered, say, a carton of smokes, three beers, and maybe a Twinkie or two—mostly for feeding a cement mixer. (I still remember the recipe: 18 shovels gravel, 9 shovels sand, 1 94-lb. bag Portland cement, 2 buckets water; mix 4 addl. mins.; pour; repeat; repeat; repeat . . . A magic elixir; it made me both strong and rich that summer.) From my post by the cement mixer, while we were building a curb around the Government Center, I once saw Haile Selassie, the Emperor of Ethiopia, who was touring the park with the Secretary of the Interior. My crew chief caught me gawking, and threatened to transfer my sorry ass to the garbage detail.

And is anybody else old enough to remember that ancient photo in the sixth-grade geography books of the two-thousand-year-old Giant Sequoia tree with the tunnel through its trunk, and a 1940 Buick convertible passing through with room to spare? Well, that summer I helped build a low stone wall right up to the mouth of that tunnel. I thought I'd left my mark upon the ages; my wall, I figured, would last at least as long as the tree, maybe another thousand years or so. But the tree came down in a terrible windstorm in 1969, and my little wall came down with it. There's probably a lesson in there somewhere on the subject of mortality—but I don't want to think about it.

During my junior year back at Miami, I had somehow contrived to get myself romantically entangled with a young lady I'll call Betsy, from up Youngstown way. She was a sweet, pretty little thing, was my Betsy, but something of a clinging vine; indeed, I must admit that it was her unprecedented enthusiasm for my physical person that had beguiled me in the first place. On the Miami campus, we'd been as inseparable as an oyster and its shell—and by the end of spring semester the oyster had begun to feel ever so slightly claustrophobic. Nonetheless, before we tore our symbiotic selves asunder for the coming summer, Betsy and I had declared ourselves "engaged to be engaged," and had received congratulations from several other bivalvular couples in our social set.

So even in Yosemite, a continent away from Youngstown, I was . . . committed. Shrouded in the mist of Bridalveil Falls, I dutifully posted Betsy's hand-tinted glamour photo above my bunk in the tent, and endeavored to compose myself for a looming eternity of wedded bliss.

However, it is written (which I know because I wrote it myself), we must never presume upon the cosmos. For example, consider this: When I arrived in the employees' village in Yosemite Valley to claim my place in tent-cabin No. 6, I discovered that the previous occupant of my bunk had left on the floor beneath it a stack of dog-eared twenty-five-cent paperback westerns and Rex Stout mysteries. But among them, improbably enough, was a first novel by a very fine writer named Bernard Malamud—a sexy, adult tale called *The Natural* about, of all things, major-league baseball.

The Natural was unlike anything I'd ever read—a very far remove indeed from the John R. Tunis sports novels of my adolescence—and I read it over and over that summer, and even allowed myself to imagine that someday I too might write such a book. But how could I have known then that only four years later, when I landed my first teaching job as a freshman comp instructor at a college in Oregon, Bernard Malamud would be one of my new colleagues, and would soon become my friend as well? Or that, after only twenty-five more years, I would publish—you guessed it—my own sexy, adult (well, sort of adult) first novel, which would be called, not altogether coincidentally, *The Natural Man*, and would be about, of all things, high school basketball.

Speaking of colleagues, my fellow inmates in our little tent-cabin ensquatment were an eclectic lot. There were probably thirty-five or forty of us, all male, of course, living four to a tent; we ate our meals in common, in a central mess hall with long, narrow tables like in boot camp or a prison, so we got to know each other pretty quickly. Perhaps as many as a third of us were college students, mostly from San Francisco and the Bay Area; the rest were relatively grizzled older guys, by and large, a raggedy-assed assortment of road-weary drifters and unskilled day laborers and farmhands up from the Central Valley between harvest seasons.

Although we all made the same egalitarian two-seventy-five an hour, there was a sort of pecking order among us, based on job description: My outfit, the road crew, was the elite, because we sometimes got to ride around in trucks up in the high country, looking for potholes, or even down in the Valley among the tourists, looking for girls. Next came the garbage crew, who also got to ride around in trucks, although they had to share the ride with stink and flies and maggots. After them came the guys who worked in the stables, tending to and cleaning up after the park rangers' horses (they got the stink and flies and maggots, but without the ride), and then the trail crew, who had to disappear into the wilderness for days at a time, and always came back aflame with poison oak.

At the bottom was the idiot-stick crew, a handful of resuscitated winos whose intellects had perhaps been compromised by their lifestyle (they patrolled the park campgrounds wielding sawed-off broomsticks with a nail in the business end, spearing bits of flotsam cast off by the tourists). The most exalted member of the latter crew was a weird old bird named Mel, who had fashioned, out of a slab of redwood and two horseshoes, a handsome rack for his idiot stick, and mounted it above his bunk, where it probably gave him more comfort than that tarted-up photo of Betsy was bringing me, of late.

The thing is, you see, I was having much too good a time out there in California, and the affectionate Betsy had lately taken to looking down upon me with the merest hint of disapproval behind her painted smile. For my life that summer wasn't all potholes and cement mixers, no indeed—because the tourist campgrounds abounded with roving bevies of predatory teenage girls bored to tears after a few days of camping out with mom and dad and that pesky little brother, and fairly spoiling for cool college guys to try their wiles upon.

Accordingly, almost every evening our little troop of cool college guys would hoof it over to Camp Curry, to let our prepossessing selves be seen. Our rate of success was indifferent at best, yet enough of my evenings culminated in lip-locks on moonlit park benches that, after a month or so, Betsy was positively glowering. Her picture, thus enhanced, soon found its way back into the suitcase beneath my bunk, and was replaced by a photo I'd clipped from that rascally new magazine *Playboy*, depicting Jayne Mansfield popping most gratifyingly out of her décolletage at some Hollywood dinner party, while Sophia Loren, seated next to her, looked on askance. I still wrote Betsy once a week, expressing my devotion, and hoped she didn't suspect that I missed the '51 Chevy Bel Air I'd left back home in Maysville a good deal more than I was missing her.

The reason I had flown to California, instead of driving the Bel Air, was that temporary employees weren't allowed to keep their cars inside the park, so I had assumed that I'd be better off without it—and besides, part of the romance of the whole enterprise lay in my plan to hitchhike home at the summer's end, one last hallelujah-I'm-a-bum adventure before the waiting tentacles of the vine-covered cottage embraced me.

But several of my new buddies, I found, had brought their cars anyhow, and left them a few miles down the road in the little town of El Portal, just outside the western entrance to the park. Now and then, one of them would hitch out to El Portal and get his wheels, so we could buy beer and drive around the park and try to pick up girls. I was always included on these excursions, not because I was much help in the picking up of girls, but because (as the result of an embarrassing little anomaly in my educational history which we needn't go into here) I was a year older than most of my peers—old enough, that is, to buy the beer, strange, exotic West Coast brands, Burgermeister and Olympia and Acme, names so intoxicating that just asking for them in the liquor store made me tipsy. Back home, we favored a Cincinnati brew called Hudepohl, which we delighted in calling Pooty Hole. It would not have done to order a Pooty Hole in California.

One weekend four or five of my new friends and I (no girls) piled into somebody's car and went all the way to Reno, where I lost two weeks' pay at the blackjack table.

Another weekend, a couple of pals from Oakland named
Jay and Tom took me home with them; we went to San
Francisco and rode the roller coaster in Luna Park, and saw
an Yma Sumac movie, and the next day we sailed under the
Golden Gate Bridge in Jay's dad's boat, and I fell in love,
ever so briefly, with Jay's exquisite older sister and—more
permanently, say for ever and ever—with San Francisco.

Among my buds from the garbage crew was a kid named
Dave, a University of Texas student from Houston who
had one of those cars in El Portal, and would be driving
home in late August. And Dave had a proposition for me: If
I'd kick in for gas and help with the driving—and buy the
beer—he said, he'd take me all the way to Houston. Now,
despite my sketchy understanding of western geography, I
had a pretty good idea of where Texas is located, but I had
to look at a map to see where on earth—where, that is, in
Texas—Houston might be. And when I realized that it happens to be situated not all that far west of New Orleans, a
port of call that would definitely add oodles of panache to
my hitchhiking itinerary, I signed on then and there. We'd
angle down through Nevada and Arizona and New Mexico
to El Paso, where, Dave proposed, we could cross the Rio
Grande into Mexico—the clincher, if I'd needed one—for
a little well-deserved R&R (Dave was a military brat) in the
fleshpots of Juarez before we headed east for Houston, and
the leading edge of the real world. Someday, I told myself,
when I got around to launching my career as a celebrated

freelance writer, I just might sit down before my Underwood in that vine-covered cottage, authorial pipe jutting from my authorial jaw, and write about this trip.

Over the course of the summer I'd managed to amass a tidy little fortune, more than three hundred bucks in cold cash. Before Dave and I left Yosemite, I pocketed fifty of it to cover travel expenses, and stashed the rest in my suitcase under Betsy's watchful eye, for the diamond engagement ring I'd promised to buy her in the fall.

Needless to say, I went back to the well a few times— more than a few—during the trip. By the time we got to Vegas, I had already discovered, in innumerable little way-side Nevada beer joints, the allure of nickel slot machines, which, nickel by nickel, depleted my capital most amazingly. In Vegas, not wanting to appear a piker, I moved on to the dime—and at last the quarter—slots, and before I knew it, I was dipping into my cash reserves again, while Betsy scowled and gnashed her teeth. In El Paso, in preparation for that little foray south of the border, I was obliged to go mano a mano with her for another withdrawal, and (international travel having proved broadening but expensive) for yet another afterward. This time, half afraid that she might bite my hand, I snatched the cash like a starving man stealing cheese from a rattrap.

Two days later, around one o'clock on a blazing August afternoon, Dave deposited me on a sun-baked stretch of highway at the eastern city limits of Houston, and left me sitting on my upended suitcase with my thumb out. At five thirty I was still sitting there, gnawing on a Baby Ruth, my poor thumb worn to a mere nub of its former self, as the rush-hour traffic streamed past, heedless and indifferent—when a well-fed Pentecostal preacher and his wife in a tiny, decrepit Henry J took pity on me, and offered me a ride to Beaumont, a whole seventy-five miles down the road. Gratefully, I climbed in. The backseat was as hard as a tombstone and as cramped as a French water closet, and the Henry J's top speed, flat out, was around thirty-five miles an hour, and the Reverend and Mrs. Quinton Hoakem, having discovered that I was a college student and surmising (quite correctly, as it happened) that I was therefore a godless sinner, grimly proselytized and sermonized me every foot of the way.

Threatening to pray assiduously for my safe passage, they dropped me off around eight thirty in the evening on the eastern outskirts of Beaumont. Reverend Hoakem was obliged to get out of the car in order to free me from his backseat. I climbed out after him, and found myself on a raised two-lane blacktop with a dismal-looking swamp on either side, near a road sign that cheerfully informed me that I was still 261 miles from New Orleans. The landscape all around us, treeless but for blighted stobs, was relentlessly flat, relieved only by tiny factories on the distant horizon belching great oily clouds of toxic fumes. The air was sultry and stifling, mephitic with swamp gas, ominously unwholesome, and swarms of mosquitoes as big as horseflies were rising from the swamp, which no doubt teemed with gators and snakes.

"Boy!" I marveled aloud as Reverend Hoakem wedged himself back into the little car. "It sure is . . . *flat* around here!"

"My son," quoth the portly divine, looking up at me from his seat behind the wheel, "she's as flat as a plate of piss."

The Reverend hooked a U-turn, and the Henry J pottered back down the empty highway toward Beaumont, into the setting sun. Glumly, I planted my suitcase on its end beside the road and sat down on it. Before the Hoakems were out of sight, I had joined them in prayer—though they were praying for my immortal soul, whereas I was just praying for a goddamn ride.

And lo, my prayers—though not the Hoakems'—were answered almost instantly. For I hadn't sat there more than three minutes when hurtling up the highway out of Beaumont came, praise His dear name, a car!

I leapt to my feet, thrust out my well-worn thumb, pasted a look of mingled hope, desperation, and old-college-try on my malleable young mug, and to my measureless delight the car slowed, then skidded to a stop a few yards beyond me. And not just any car, either, no dinky little four-horse Henry J this time, but an Olds 88 two-door hardtop, new as daybreak, cherry-red and white, with whitewalls and fender skirts and more chrome than a mobster's casket, and the windows opened all the way back to cool the ride, verily a creampuff, a heaven-sent dreamboat. As I grabbed my suitcase and hurried toward it, a balding, one-armed gent in a Hawaiian shirt stepped out on the passenger side.

"Hop in, Slick," he said amiably, holding the door open with the only hand he had, the right, which also held a can of beer.

Ecstatic, I heaved my suitcase into the backseat and climbed in after it, ready to go wherever this deus ex machina would take me. While I got in, the one-armed man, holding his beer telephone-style between his jaw and his shoulder, availed himself of the opportunity to step to the roadside and take a leak, which allowed me a moment to size up my new circumstances.

The car's only other occupant was a redheaded woman at the wheel, a real looker, an eyeful, I noted, despite (or maybe to some extent because of) rhinestone-studded cat's-eye shades and a prodigious quantity of makeup. To protect her flaming auburn coif from the wind, she wore a green scarf tied at the back of her neck, a style which for whatever reason reminded me of Susan Hayward, who to my post-teenage libido represented the very pinnacle of ambition. She had the road-weary but still dangerous look of a woman who had seen a lot . . . and had perhaps been seen a good deal as well—in short, a regular floozy, as my mom (and your mom) would've said.

Just now the Regular Floozy was impatiently tapping the

accelerator and drumming her ruby-red fingernails on the horn-ring and darting menacing sidelong glances at her traveling companion, who, circumstanced as he unfortunately chanced to be in the matter of available digits, was apparently having trouble buttoning up.

"F'crissakes, Chick!" she snapped, racing the motor. "Hurry up and put it away, will ya!"

Chick, still fumbling at his fly, obediently crept back into the car. "Aw now, Fondelle, baby, you know I—" he began, but the lady thus denominated slammed the accelerator to the floor and scratched off, fishtailing up the road while he was still trying to close the car door.

That accomplished, Chick turned to me with a sheepish grin. "Fondelle's in a big hurry, see. 'Cause her and me is headed to New Orleans to get married. She can't hardly wait," he chortled, "can you, baby?"

"That's right," Fondelle said, through clenched teeth. "I can't wait. Hardly." She viciously punched in the cigarette lighter, fished a Pall Mall from the purse on the seat beside her, and fired it up. "Where you headed, boy?" she flung back at me over her shoulder, the words, accompanied by a streaming plume of cigarette smoke, riding the blessed cool air rushing in through the windows.

"WELL, ACTUALLY." I shouted into the wind, "I WAS KIND OF GOING TO NEW ORLEANS MYSELF, MA'AM. SEE, I—"

"You're a lucky boy, then," she said. And those were the

last words she addressed to me for the ensuing hundred miles.

But Chick proved much more communicative. "Chick Brewster is my name," he said, extending his hand to me over the back of the seat, "and Arbuckle, Oklahoma, is my station. Now Fondelle here," he added proudly, "she's from New York City, New York!"

Trying hard to forget Chick's recent difficulties in responding to that call of nature, I reluctantly shook his hand—and as I did, realizing that he was waiting for me to complete the round of introductions, I heard myself whoop, to my own utter astonishment, at the top of my windblown voice:

"HOWDY! I'M . . . STERLING PRIEST!"

It was the name I had decided back in high school would be my nom de plume if I ever managed to become a writer. But why I chose to haul it out that night for Chick and Fondelle—for the first and only time in all my life, before or since—remains a perfect mystery to me even now, after almost fifty years. I was pretty sure that when I said the name I saw, in the darkening rearview mirror as we sped along, the shadow of a knowing smirk cross Fondelle's face.

"So, Squirrelly," Chick inquired, pausing to take a long pull at his beer, "are you a married man?"

Me? A married man? "NO!" I shouted. Immediately, Betsy's image rose up out of the suitcase on the seat beside me, like a genie from a bottle, grim and scowling. "BUT I'M ENGAGED!" I added hastily, and Betsy vanished as swiftly as she'd come.

"Well, that's good, Squirrelly, that's good," Chick assured me, leaning intimately over the back of his seat. ("Sterling," I objected feebly, but Chick didn't seem to notice.) "Me and Fondelle has been engaged since day before yesterday ourself! This little lady is gonna set Arbuckle a-fahr, buddy-ro!"

I declared, as assertively as I could, that I didn't doubt it for a minute.

"Fondelle, doll baby," Chick said, "lemme show Squirrelly that newspaper." Fondelle shrugged her indifference to the proposition, and Chick passed me a well-worn clipping of a grainy photo from a New York tabloid, datelined about a year earlier, of four people, three men and a woman, gathered over drinks around a table in what appeared, judging by the potted palm trees and the scantily clad cigarette girl in the background, to be a swanky nightclub. I recognized the gents right away: Leo Durocher, Walter Winchell, and Jack Dempsey. The woman—a real eyeful—was intriguingly familiar too, but I had to look twice before it came to me that she was, in absolute fact, Fondelle.

"BUSMAN'S HOLIDAY," read the caption. "Prominent restaurateur and former heavyweight champ Jack Dempsey, and his date, Manhattan showgirl Fondelle Fontaine, share a table at the Stork Club with Dodger manager Leo Durocher and columnist Walter Winchell."

"Gosh!" I cried, upwind. "Jack Dempsey!"

Chick probably hadn't heard me, but he caught my drift. "Ain't she a pip!" he exulted. "Ain't she a goddamn pistol!" He drained the last of his beer, pitched the empty out the window, and, reaching somewhere beneath his seat, came up with a full pint of hundred-proof Wild Turkey. He clamped the bottle between his knees, twisted off the cap, took a slug, and turned to offer it to me—but Fondelle quickly put the quietus on my hopes by smacking his hand and observing that one shit-faced drunk in the car at a time was as many as she could stand.

Maybe even one more than she could stand. It was beginning to occur to me, dimly, that the reason Fondelle had picked me up in the first place was that, after three long days of prenuptial togetherness, she was sick and tired of being Chick's only audience; maybe she still had to hear him, but at least she didn't have to listen to him. From here on, that would be my job—which meant that I'd need to stay upright and vaguely sentient (hence no Wild Turkey) at least as long as Chick did.

Chick proved an indefatigable if not wonderfully scintillating conversationalist, so all I had to do, really, was settle back in my seat and holler an occasional "REALLY!" or "GOSH!" or "IZZAT SO?" and otherwise let him carry the load, while Fondelle drove and smoked and cracked her gum and listened to loud, scratchy pop music on the radio.

Over the next couple of hours, as night fell and we plunged on through the black Louisiana swamplands, I learned that Chick was the Standard Oil distributor in Arbuckle, county seat of Trench County and home of the World's Largest Hog-

Ring Factory (I made a feeble attempt at interjecting here the equally interesting fact that Maysville, *my* hometown, boasted the World's Largest Pulley Factory, but Arbuckle had the floor, and wouldn't yield), and that as a Purple Heart veteran of World War II—he lost the arm to a land mine at Anzio—yours truly Chick Brewster was much honored and highly regarded amongst your finest hoi polloi of Arbuckle, and was on a first-name basis with the absolute owner of the hog-ring factory. Wherever he went in Arbuckle, Chick asserted with a sly chuckle, folks would say, "Here comes Chickie with his Purple Heart on!" So when Chick Brewster brought his new bride home to Arbuckle—and here he laid his hand on Fondelle's shoulder in a proprietary manner, but she savagely brushed it off, as though it were some loathsome swampy thing that had flown in through the window—those fine folks were gonna treat the little lady like a goddamn queen!

"Yeah, that's me," Fondelle muttered. "The Purple Hard-On Queen of Arbuckle, Oklahoma."

But Chick was too busy talking to notice the aside. As he rattled on—and on, and on—I availed myself of the opportunity to contemplate at my leisure the happy prospect of spending a couple of exciting days in New Orleans, which according to my understanding was populated exclusively by artists and bohemians, similar to the ones I'd read about in the Henry Miller novels I'd smuggled in from my week in Paris the previous summer. I was anxious to get a look at some artists and bohemians for myself, and I figured I'd better do it pretty quick, because I was reasonably sure that Betsy wasn't partial to the type.

Chick had a whiney, adenoidal voice and a Fuller Brush man's way of insistently boring in on his listener, which I soon discovered (like Fondelle before me) made it almost impossible to ignore him. He had come to Dallas, he told me between snorts from the pint, for a convention of highway contractors who were about to get rich on all those new interstates the government was planning to punch through. The legislation hadn't even passed yet, but blue-ribbon commissions and congressional committees had been formed, and rumors were flying. The very first stretch would be inflicted upon the state of Oklahoma, reliable sources held, and behind the scenes the money was already flowing.

Naturally the convention hotel had been swarming with politicians and heavy-equipment salesmen and union people and materials suppliers and small-time deal makers like my excellent new friend Chick, who was looking for palms to grease in hopes of getting the bid to supply petroleum products to whichever outfits were to build the stretch of interstate that was sure to pass through Trench County. On the first day of the convention he bought one congressman a two-hundred-dollar suit of clothes and another dedicated public servant a case of whiskey; the second day cost him a Harris Tweed sport coat, plus porterhouse steak dinners for a party of six contractors. It was an exshpensive way to do business, Chick acknowledged with a grand flourish of the now half-empty pint, but you gotta shpend money to make money.

That philosophy was shared by the big shpenders who'd put the convention together, and were so flush with future prosperity that they'd decided to enliven the proceedings by flying in a planeload of "hostesses" from New York City — which was where Fondelle came in. Chick met her when she served him a drink while he was shooting craps — and trying hard not to win — in a hotel room with a bunch of contractors and politicians. They fell in love on the spot, Chick assured me, and the next day he proved his love by buying her the Olds 88.

"She won't even let me set behind the wheel," he giggled, "willya, baby? You won't even let sweet daddy dwive your widdle tar, willums, baby doll?" By this point in his narrative, Chick was getting pretty loose. Several times along the way, he'd appealed, in baby talk, to Fondelle's affectionate nature, and each time she'd replied with a monosyllabic grunt. This time, though, she had a rather more emphatic response:

"You bet your one-armed ass I won't!"

Abruptly, she wheeled the Olds into an all-night gas station and diner. It was around midnight, and we were on the outskirts of Lafayette, Louisiana. Fondelle told the attendant to fill it up, and marched off to the ladies' room. Chick more or less fell out of the car, stuffed the pint into his hip pocket, and lurched away toward the gents' facility. Like Fondelle, I too was growing a little weary of Chick's loquacious company, but nature obliged me to follow him in, and join him at the reverse watering trough. As before, Chick was having some difficulty dealing with the mechanics of the operation, which gave him ample opportunity to buttonhole me—figuratively speaking—for further inebrious fraternization.

"So tell me, Shquirrelly," he inquired, "you got a shoot in that shoo—s-s-suitcase of yours?"

Chick's articulation—especially in regard to the sibilants—was rapidly deteriorating (although his voice was no less annoying for that), and when he directed his question to me, the Wild Turkey fumes overwhelmed even the breath-stopping reek of the hockey-puck disinfectant discs in the urinal.

But as a matter of improbable fact, I did have a suit—a snappy little seersucker number, complete with a white, short-sleeved, button-down wash-and-wear shirt and a skinny rep-stripe tie in the charcoal-and-pink combo that was all the rage that year on college campuses. I can't imagine what earthly use I'd supposed I was going to have for this getup on a road crew in Yosemite; nonetheless, there it was, still stuffed away in my suitcase, exactly where it had been since I carefully packed it there last June.

Sure, I told Chick, I've got a suit. But why do you ask?

Chick wasn't tracking too good, conversation-wise, but he had a proposition in mind, and he resolutely pulled himself together and laid it on me. Why, he said, he was thinking maybe I could stand up with him when he and Fondelle got married tomorrow. Because he didn't know nobody in New Orleans, and he didn't want some damn shtranger (which, it crossed my mind, described me to a tee) as his best man. Now Fondelle, Chick went boozily on, she had a girlfriend there, a real pretty girl named, uh, Mary, yeah, that was her name, Mary, beautiful girl, who'd be standing up with her, and after the wedding we'd go out and drink champagne and all. And who knows, maybe Mary and I—beautiful girl, Mary, just a beautiful girl, and when she got a loada me decked out in my sh-suit and all, who knows, maybe we'd hit it off and get married too, and we'd all go back to Arbuckle and he'd set Mary and me up in a nice little house and give me a job driving one of his tank trucks, because there'd be big money to be made in Arbuckle when this new intershta— interstate goes through. So tomorrow morning his people back in Oklahoma would be wiring him some cash, a thousand or two for his honeymoon, y'know, the boss's honeymoon. In the meantime, though, he was a little short, because Fondelle, she was the banker in this outfit, she had charge of all the dough, heh heh, and he was a little short of pocket money. So—just till tomorrow morning, Shquirrelly, when the wire comes in—maybe I could let him have . . . twenty dollars?

By this time Chick had at last mastered the intricacies of his fly, and now he stood before me, swaying a bit unsteadily on his feet, his (only) hand extended, making that imperious little *c'mon, gimme* gesture with his thumb and fingertips, as though I owed him the twenty dollars. And simpleton that I was, temporarily under an enchantment, mesmerized by the shining image of the gorgeous, hitherto unimagined Mary and a wildly erotic future with her in Arbuckle, Oklahoma, a non-Betsy future that I hadn't even dreamed of two minutes ago, I forked it over.

We caught up with Fondelle in the diner, sitting in a booth drinking coffee and smoking impatiently. She didn't look wonderfully pleased to see us. I was famished — except for that Baby Ruth and the pack of Nabs I'd scarfed when Reverend Hoakem stopped for gas many hours ago, I hadn't eaten a bite since lunch — so I ordered two grilled cheese sandwiches and a chocolate shake. Chick asked for a cup of coffee and, as soon as the waitress delivered it and turned her back, slipped his pint out of his hip pocket, clamped it into his left armpit by means of the stump inside his shirtsleeve, deftly unscrewed the top, and added a generous dollop to his coffee.

"Jee-zus Christ," Fondelle said, with palpable disgust.

"Aw, baby," Chick whined, "my stump's a-hurting me!"

"Good," she muttered through her teeth.

Chick tried a different tack. "So guess what, shweetheart, Squirrelly's gonna stand up wimme! He's got a suit an' all!"

"Whoop-de-doo," rejoiced the bride-to-be.

I longed to ask Fondelle to tell me about her sublime friend Mary, but she was clearly in no mood to discuss anything related to the forthcoming hymeneal rites. I also had a burning desire to know just what it is that a Manhattan showgirl *does*, exactly, but that question didn't seem quite politic either. So I asked her instead what Jack Dempsey was really like.

"Jack's a real sweetie," she said almost wistfully, with a scornful glance at her fiancé, who had collapsed, more or less insensate, in the seat beside her as if he'd sprung a leak, and was slowly deflating. "Jack knows how to treat a girl."

What about Leo Durocher and Walter Winchell?

"Horses' asses," Fondelle said, without equivocation. "Two royal horses' asses."

The waitress, who serendipitously arrived just then with my order and no doubt thought Fondelle was referring to Chick and me, rolled her eyes and murmured, "I'll say," as she set my sandwiches before me.

Fondelle, clickety-clicking her alarmingly red fingernails on the tabletop, told me to eat the hell up, she wanted to get the hell on the road. Nonetheless, my questions about her illustrious connections had evidently rendered her a bit more talkative. While I was bolting my sandwiches, she volunteered that she had "worked" lots of conventions in New Orleans (I was beginning to get a better idea of what a showgirl does for a living), and that she knew her way around the city like Carter knows Little Liver Pills. She always stayed at the Monteleone, she said, which she gave me to understand was the ritziest hotel in the French Quarter.

Emboldened, I asked whether she happened to know of any not-so-ritzy hotels in the neighborhood. Yeah, Fondelle said, there was a place on Canal, eight bucks a night, just around the corner from the quarter. In fact, she added, Goldilocks here—she meant Chick, who was by now thoroughly comatose, and blowing spit-bubbles with every snore— Goldilocks here would be staying there himself tonight, although he didn't know it yet. Because she was gonna be dog-tired by the time we got to New Orleans—hell, she was dog-tired *now*—she needed her beauty sleep, and she did not have no intention whatsoever to spend another night in a wrestling match with a damned one-armed dipso.

It was just at that exact moment, as I was stuffing the last bite of my third triangular half of a grilled cheese sandwich into my mouth, that I fell utterly and irretrievably in love. Now the attentive reader may have observed that I tended, at that period of my young life, to fall in love rather readily: In addition to the omnipresent Betsy and her bevy of predecessors, there had been, in rapid succession, two or three teenage Yosemite nymphets, Jayne Mansfield (a mere dalliance), my friend Jay's lovely sister in Oakland, a couple more nymphets back in Yosemite, a dark-eyed señorita by the name of Marta in Juarez just three days ago (who, I was to discover a few days later, had presented me with a small but rapidly multiplying family of tiny migrant stowaways), and finally, only fifteen or twenty minutes ago, Mary, the goddess who quite possibly existed only in my own fevered imagination and in the wily machinations of a one-armed, stone-drunk Standard Oil distributor from Arbuckle, Oklahoma.

Nonetheless, in love I absolutely was . . . again. Fondelle had long since put aside her shades, and she was certainly dog-tired; there was a sort of bruised look about her eyes, part weariness and part smeared mascara, that spoke to me of experience, of worldliness, of ill-usage and ruin, of com-mingled toughness and vulnerability. It made me think of that Rita Hayworth line—"Armies have marched over me!"—in *Miss Sadie Thompson*, still the sexiest line ever uttered on the screen. Fondelle was older than I'd thought, maybe thirty-five or so—but that only added a certain poi-gnancy to her mystique. My heart welled with tenderness and desire; I would dedicate my youthful vigor to comforting her as she slipped almost imperceptibly into early middle age, coughed consumptively a few times, and expired in my arms. Afterward, I told myself as I slurped the dregs of my chocolate shake, I would carry on somehow. But first, I had to make my move.

"So, um, Fondelle," I purred, lowering my voice to its most suavay, most seductively continental tone, "tell me, is Manhattan right *in* New York City, or is it in the suburbs?"

For the first time all evening, Fondelle cracked a smile, then she snickered, then she snorted coffee through her nose. "Hell's bells," she said, still laughing as she policed herself up with a paper napkin, "you're green as grass, kiddo!"

(I was beginning to notice, by the way, that Fondelle's inflections—"Hail's bails, yore grain as grace!"—smacked more of my own neck of the woods than of New York City. I was clearly no expert on matters Manhattan, but I could recognize an Upper Ohio Valley twang when I heard one.)

Fondelle turned to Chick and punched him pretty smartly on the shoulder. "Wake up, sunbeam," she said. "Let's make like a sewer and get the shit outta here."

Together, she and I steered the mumbling, stumbling Chick out of the diner and back to the car, where Fondelle summarily confiscated the remains of the pint of Wild Turkey and ordered Chick to take my place in the backseat and sleep it off. Settling herself behind the wheel, she put the Wild Turkey on the seat between us and told me, as she wheeled the 88 back out onto the highway, that I could finish it off if I wanted. Guiltily, I glanced back at Chick, but he was already dead to the world—and anyhow, I saw when I held the jug up to the light, there was only one pretty good belt left. So as soon as Fondelle had us rolling again, I knocked it back, a double shot of Ole Liquid-Plumr that went down like swallowing a hot poker. Following Chick's example, I chucked the empty out into the Louisiana night, and sat back to take the evening airs.

———

I awoke when Fondelle pulled to a stop in front of a small Canal Street hotel — I don't recall the name, so let's call it the Metropole — and began rather abrasively admonishing Chick and me to wake the hail up and get the hail out of the car, it was two thirty in the morning and she needed to get the hail to sleep. As we groggily disembarked, Chick whined quite piteously to the effect that he was being denied his last night of nonconjugal bliss, but Fondelle was unmoved. Nothing doing, she said; he had already drove that into the ground and broke it off. She dug a ten-dollar bill out of her purse and gave it to Chick for his hotel room, and left us standing beside our suitcases in front of the seedy old Metropole, blinking in the neon glare of countless Canal Street we-never-close bars. Despite the lateness of the hour, the sidewalks were crowded with pedestrians, mostly drunken gents in fezzes — a Shriners' convention was evidently in town — many a bemused and fezz-betopped gent with his own personal Manhattan Showgirl on his arm. It was all strangely disorienting, as if I'd been suddenly dropped down into the middle of the Casbah.

"I don't hardly feel like hittin' the hay right now," Chick said when the 88's taillights had merged into the late-night Canal Street traffic. He looked off down the street where, in the middle of the next block, I could see the familiar animated sign of the eternally galloping neon Greyhound. "What say me and you run down here to the Long Dog and stow our gear in a locker, and go out and have us a little drink?"

I couldn't make it, I told him; it had been a long day, and I was bushed. Chick wasn't looking so hot himself: his Hawaiian shirt was as rumpled as a fruit salad, his face was ashen and stubbly, and his eyes, in the words of the old song, looked like two cherries in a glass of buttermilk. He promised vaguely that he'd see me tomorrow, then, and picked up his suitcase and started off down Canal Street.

"Hey, Chick!" I called after him. "What time's the wedding?"

He stopped in his tracks, hesitated for a long moment as if pondering his answer, then glanced back over his armless shoulder. "Uh, three o'clock," he said, already moving on. "Three o'clock sharp."

And there went Chickie with his Purple Heart on. Listing hard to the right, struggling to counterbalance the weight of the suitcase with the arm that wasn't there, he soldiered on down Canal, looking terribly, touchingly alone and forlorn. Sadly, that was to be the last I'd ever see of him — or, needless to say, of my twenty dollars.

But of course I didn't know that then, and thus I awoke the following morning in my tiny, stifling hotel room, filled with a powerful sense of purpose: I had to get to a dry cleaner right away, to have my seersucker suit pressed for the wedding! Ah, and for Mary!

Hastily, I washed up at the sink in my room (in the Metropole the bathrooms were, as the night clerk had told me when I checked in, "conveniently located down the hall"), got dressed, and set out with my shapeless wad of crumpled seersucker in search of an establishment that could coax it back to life. I inquired of the ancient black gentleman in the rusty-looking call-for-Phillip-Morris livery who operated the Metropole's rickety elevator (and who had been there when I checked in last night, and was still there this morning, and would be there every time I came and went for the next twenty-four hours, and for all I know absolutely resided in the elevator, like some garrulous old raven in a relentlessly upsy-downsy cage)—and Old Bikey (as he called himself) directed me and my seersucker bolus to a Chinese laundry a few blocks down Canal.

I paused at the desk to inquire whether a one-armed party by the name of C. Brewster had checked in, and was informed that no person of that description had been seen or heard of. Okay, I figured, maybe he weaseled his way into Fondelle's bed in the Monteleone after all, or had enjoyed his little drink or three and then slept it off in the Greyhound station. On the way to the laundry, I popped into the Long Dog and looked around, fruitlessly, for a snoozing Chick, and even asked a porter whether he'd seen my distinctive one-armed friend; he hadn't, the porter said, but then he was on the day shift, and the night shift had gone home a couple of hours ago. So, following Old Bikey's directions, I hoofed it on down Canal, deposited my suit at the No Tickee No Washee, and sallied forth into the French Quarter to take me a gander at some of them bohemians.

The bohos, I discovered, weren't necessarily early risers; I wandered about amongst throngs of tourists for quite a while without spotting a single one. With the impending nuptials in mind, I treated myself to a shoe-shine administered by a grinning urchin whom I tipped a shiny new fifty-cent piece, doing so with a magisterial air that befit my status as best-man-to-be. Then I manfully downed a cup of chickory-laced tarwater in a sidewalk coffee shop, watched a profusely sweating one-man band's futile effort to make "When the Saints Go Marching In" fresh and scintillating, ate (against my better judgment) a fried-oyster po'boy on a park bench in Jackson Square . . . and, all the while, I kept one eye out for artistic types, and the other out for Chick.

The latter sighting never happened, but I did finally come upon a guy with a beret and a goatee and an artist's smock, parked on the sidewalk on Dauphine Street with an easel before him, executing overpriced charcoal caricatures of susceptible tourists. I stood there looking over his shoulder for a few minutes, contemplating my Betsy's unalloyed delight when I returned to her with a handsome portrait of handsome Me destined to hang in some prime location in our vine-covered cottage—or, on the other hand, whether the divine Mary mightn't appreciate it even more when she and I installed the masterpiece in our little love nest out there in Arbuckle, Oklahoma. Unfortunately, the caricatures themselves were uniformly so inept, so mean, and so ugly that I couldn't quite see the efficacy of paying myself that particular homage, especially since it would've cost me twenty bucks to be thus immortalized. So I moved along.

I picked up my suit around one o'clock and, on my way back to the Metropole, peeked in at the Greyhound station one more time. No sign of Chick. At the Metropole, I inquired at the desk whether Sterling Priest had had any calls, and was informed that he had not. Delivered upstairs by the ever-faithful Old Bikey, I found the bathroom down the hall available, and locked myself in for a long, much-needed shower. Back in my room, I laid out my freshly pressed suit, my short-sleeved button-down shirt, my rep-striped tie, and my newly shined cordovans, shaved my meager whiskers at the sink, slapped my callow cheeks vigorously with copious quantities of Mennen Skin Bracer, applied a whopping great glob of Wildroot Creme Oil to my unruly locks, dressed myself with care, observed at length my much-improved image in the shaving mirror, and at last determined myself ready to undertake my assignment.

When I stepped onto the elevator, Bikey rolled his rheumy old eyes at me and whistled softly under his breath and said, "Whoo-ee!" These compliments cost me another fifty-cent gratuity, but they were worth every penny of it; I sauntered out of the Metropole and strolled down through the Quarter to the Monteleone (again following Old Bikey's directions) feeling every inch the pluperfect Best Man.

The Monteleone's lobby, small but elegantly appointed, fairly swarmed with fezzes and showgirls. Seeing no sign of my wedding party, I peeked into the bar—it was called the Carousel—but they weren't there either. So I turned back to the lobby and located, between a potted palm and an elephant ear, an unoccupied (and, it soon developed, excruciatingly uncomfortable) Louis Quatorze chair which commanded a view of, at once, the front door, the elevator, and the entrance to the Carousel, wherein a brisk trade was transpiring even though it was only three o'clock in the afternoon.

Three fifteen came and went and was followed, in due time, by three thirty and three forty-five—and still no Chick and Fondelle. Lovely ladies came and went the whole time, beauteous young things, any one of whom could have been—but evidently wasn't—the Mary of my dreams, while I squirmed and sweated, much to the disadvantage of my suit, on this chair that Louis of Yore must have intended for his torture chamber. Inside the Carousel, the actual bar itself, a circular affair in the center of the room, was slowly, almost imperceptibly rotating in a clockwise direction, a strangely disagreeable phenomenon, even from afar. I couldn't help wondering if that oyster po'boy was finally checking in on me.

Along about four o'clock, a beefy, unaccommodating sort in an ill-fitting brown suit approached me and, addressing me as "Sir" in a growling, insinuating tone, inquired whether I was "expected" by a guest of the establishment. Now I had read enough cheesy detective fiction out there in my bunk in Yosemite to know that this hard-boiled party with the ugly squint was what I had learned to call a House Dick; so I says, Yessir, I am, heh heh, but maybe I'll just step over here to the desk and see if my party's been, um, detained. Why don't you do that, says he. Okay, says I; okay, okay.

Under the house dick's watchful eye, I sidled up to the desk and asked the clerk to ring Miss Fontaine's room on the house phone. He consulted his guest ledger with the most perfunctory of glances, then looked down his supercilious nose and assured me that no Miss Fontaine was registered there, and wondered aloud whether I might possibly have the wrong hotel.

Surely there must be some mistake, I implored. Fondelle Fontaine? From Manhattan, in New York City? Redhead? A real . . . a real eyeful?

"Sonny," said the clerk, languidly closing his book, "there are probably at least a dozen ladies of that description in this hotel right this very minute."

Baffled and disheartened, I turned to slink away, when suddenly the elevator doors slid open and, like the cover of one of those dog-eared Yosemite paperbacks—say, *The Case of the Purple Hard-On*, by Celebrated Freelance Author Squirrelly Priest—out stepped Fondelle herself: white stiletto heels, black net hose, skintight black sheath dress, dangerous décolletage, the familiar cat's-eye shades, auburn hair spilling like molten copper from beneath a huge white picture hat . . .

"Hail's bails," she murmured, drawing up short when she saw me standing there amidst the potted flora of the lobby, with floozies and fezzes passing to and fro about us like butterflies and hookah-smoking caterpillars, "look what the cat drug in." Clearly, she'd forgotten that I existed.

"Fondelle!" I said. "Where's Chick?"

She glanced warily around the lobby. "He ain't *here*?"

For the longest, stupidest moment, I thought she was about to lambaste me for having failed, as best man, to deliver the groom. Then I realized that what alarmed her was exactly the opposite possibility.

No no, I assured her, he went out drinking last night and never came back to the hotel.

Fondelle was visibly relieved. "You wait right here (rye cheer) a minute," she said. She turned and sashayed over to the desk where, out of earshot, she chatted briefly with the clerk, with whom she appeared to be on familiar terms. He responded, laughing and rolling his eyes; then he glanced at me, rolled his eyes again, and they both laughed. She came back and, without a word, took me by the elbow and steered me into the Carousel.

The dyspeptic house dick had posted himself like a scowling, squinting Cerberus by the door, next to a potted palm. As we walked by, Fondelle greeted him with a wave and a breezy "How ya doin', Eugene!" and he responded with a grin so huge it threatened to shatter his stony visage. "Hi'ya, Miss Fontaine!" he said warmly. At the Monteleone, Fondelle was indisputably a member of the family.

We found seats at the circular bar amongst the assembled revelers, and Fondelle asked the bartender (she called him Bob) to bring us two Sazeracs. I had no idea what a Sazerac might consist of, but the name fairly reeked of dissolution and debauchery, so I was hopeful. No telling what-all might be in it. According to my sources, you could get just about anything you wanted in New Orleans—and hadn't I seen a place called the Old Absinthe House in the French Quarter that very morning? Absinthe? It was too much to wish for.

When our drinks arrived, I made as if to pay up, but Fondelle said I should put my money away, and told Bob to start a tab for her. In the backbar mirror, I saw her treat Bob to a sly but knowing wink behind her shades. He grinned and said, "Sure thing, Fondelle," and lit her Pall Mall with a dexterous flip of his Zippo.

"Don't worry about it, hon," she said when he was gone. "Bob's run many a tab for me, and I ain't paid one yet."

"So . . . where's Chick?"

"On his way home to Arbuckle," Fondelle answered with one of her expressive shrugs, "I most sincerely goddamn hope."

The Sazerac turned out to be a tea-colored potion in a tall glass. When I raised it to my lips, it gave off a faint effluvia of . . . licorice! And when with my first cautious sip I detected a subtle but distinct understatement of Black Jack chewing gum, my darkest suspicions were confirmed. Absinthe, sure as hell! Was Fondelle plying me with intoxicating liquors in order to lure me up to her hotel room and use me horribly? I most sincerely goddamn hoped so!

Whatever her motives, Fondelle was proving a lot more sociable than she'd been last night—and a great deal more forthcoming. Indeed, she was eagerly telling me the whole story:

When she first hooked up with Chick back in Dallas (she was saying, sounding less like Manhattan and more like West Virginia with every syllable), she'd thought he was actually sort of cute, y'know, for a one-armed guy. He was trying to act like a big shot, of course, she could see that; still, he was sweet and generous, spending his money like there wasn't no tomorrow and introducing her to everybody as the future Mrs. Brewster. Which at first she thought that was just the usual line of bull, but then when he went and bought her that Olds 88, she told herself, Well, hell (Wail, hail), I could do this. I could be Mrs. Chick Brewster, and play canasta with the high uppity-ups out in Arbuckle, Oklahoma. And besides, a one-armed man ought to be easier to handle than a regular one, even if he did have a Purple Heart and a Standard Oil dealership.

(The roisterous presence of all those celebratory Shriners and showgirls gathered about the bar was imposing a certain intimacy upon us: Fondelle's lovely, delicately ravaged countenance was but a heavy breath away. Trembling within, confident only that my barstool stood poised on the

brink of perdition, I ventured a second sip of my Sazerac —
and then a third, and eventually a fourth. The creeping rota-
tion of the bar was faintly nauseating; I felt ever so slightly
giddy, fuzzled, as though the absinthe were already going
to my head. The panoramic mural of the French Quarter
that lined the walls of the room crawled along, clockwise,
at about the pace of a really tedious carriage ride. It was
enough to make a person swear off absinthe altogether.)

But hon (Fondelle went on), the guy was so full of it! He
would talk the hind leg off a dog, him and that dentist-drill
voice of his. They wasn't two hours out of Dallas yesterday
morning till she felt like she had met half the people in
Arbuckle, and hoped to God she never met the other half.
Because once a person has been out on a date with Jack
Dempsey, she's just not gonna be all that impressed by a hog-
ring manufacturer. She didn't run off from West Virginia,
Fondelle declared, just to get talked to a frazzle in the state
of Oklahoma.

So when she picked me up last night, she said, I was
just what the doctor ordered; with me on board for Chick
to talk to, and the radio turned up loud, she could finally
hear herself think. And what she mostly heard, listening to
herself think, was that she did not intend to marry this one-
armed dipso under no circumstances whatsoever, not in no
way, shape, form, manner, or means, period, end of story.
She had already been married to several dipsos, and had
not enjoyed it one bit. The problem was how to get shed of

this one and get her ass to New Orleans without having to marry him. She would've drove off and left Chick and me in that filling station men's room, except she just hadn't been raised that way.

Any-hoo (Fondelle continued, shifting gears), by the time we got to New Orleans she had it all doped out. After she ditched us at the Metropole, she had went straight to the Monteleone—where, I might've noticed, she's well-known—and parked the 88 in the hotel garage. At the front desk she asked Artie, the night clerk, for an envelope, and in the envelope she put the car keys and the title and the garage parking stub, and sealed the envelope and wrote Chick's name on it and gave it back to Artie. Tomorrow morning, she told him, a certain one-armed john is gonna come around asking for Fondelle Fontaine, and I want Wally (which that was Wally out there right now, the day clerk, the guy she was just talking to), I want Wally to give this to him and tell him that Miss Fontaine was, uh, that she was called out of town on urgent business, and wouldn't be coming back.

And then, Fondelle said, she checked in under her real name, Arletta Skeens, and slipped Artie two fivers—one for him and one for Wally—and went up to her room and crawled into bed and slept till two o'clock this afternoon.

The absinthe had rendered me almost speechless, but I managed to croak, "Arletta Skeens?"

"That's right," said Fondelle Fontaine, with yet another sly but knowing wink, just between us impostors. "That's right, Sterling Priest. "

"Actually," I admitted sheepishly, "it's Eddie McCla—um, Ed McClanahan." Hoping to redeem some tiny smidgeon of my dignity, I added, "Sterling Priest is just my, um, pen name."

If Fondelle—I wasn't quite ready for Arletta Skeens—if Fondelle had the foggiest notion what on earth a pen name might be (the name I went by when I was in the pen, maybe?), she didn't let on. She just shrugged again, as if to say, Well, either way, it's a poor out for a name, and went on with her story.

"See," she confided, speaking with renewed urgency, "I *coultn't* keep the man's car. I mean, he's a damn war hero, hon! I lost my daddy in that old war." She sniffled, lifted her shades, and dabbed a tear in the corner of her eye. "I just kinda, you know, took a notion."

Exit Fondelle Fontaine, Manhattan Showgirl, consort to the stars, heartless gold digger. A fond farewell to the fair Fondelle. Enter Arletta Skeens, good ol' gal from West Virginia, who had took a notion. And now I saw at last why she had been so eager to tell me the story—because she had done a great thing, Arletta had, something fine and grand and noble and self-sacrificing, and I, this wet-behind-the-ears hayseed best man in the rumpled seersucker suit, was perhaps the only person in all the living world who could fully appreciate the magnitude of the deed—the only person, for that matter, who would even believe it, ladies in the gold-digging line not being in the habit, ordinarily, of refunding Olds 88s to rejected admirers.

"But I ditn't wanna be married to him for the rest of my damn life, neither," Arletta said, with a little shudder. "Not under no circumstances whatsoever."

Afterward, whenever (increasingly infrequent) thoughts of the waiting arms of Betsy crossed my mind, I would remember that little involuntary shudder of Arletta's, and experience my own tiny tremor of pre-connubial dread.

Just at the present moment, however, I was lost in a reverie of an entirely different description: I found myself staring straight down into the alluring depths of Arletta's cleavage, and in my absinthe-inflamed imagination I was transported to somewhere in the mountains of West Virginia, scaling snowy peaks.

Not surprisingly, I was a little slow in realizing that Arletta had just spoken to me. "Watch out now," she'd cautioned, with a generous giggle. "Don't fall in."

I raised my eyes and saw my guilty blush light up the backbar mirror. But Arletta's enterprising attention had already turned to the business at hand.

"God amighty!" she exclaimed, surveying the roomful of schooling conventioneers as though she were casting an invisible net, and calculating in advance the weight of the catch. "This place is broke out in Shriners! You better drink up on your cocktail, hon. I've got a date with . . . somebody."

She said the last almost tenderly, yet all my instincts told me that my idyll in the West Virginia hills was over. Feeling like I was about nine years old, I clambered down from my barstool and drew myself up to my full, seersuckered nine-year-old height and thanked her politely for the lift and the Sazerac cocktail (the effects of which were rapidly evaporating). She kissed me soundly on the cheek and instructed me to be sure and have a good time in New Orleans, now, and not do nothing she woultn't do.

I stopped in the men's room, and when I came out I saw that there were two Shrinies in close conversation with her, one on either side, the tops of their fezzes peeping like bashful mushrooms from behind her picture hat. Possibly they were vying to determine which one got the privilege of paying her (and my) bar tab. Despite her shades, I caught Arletta's eye in the backbar mirror, and we exchanged diffident little farewell salutes. Out in the street, I realized that I'd forgotten to ask whether she happened to have a girlfriend named Mary—but I was pretty sure I knew what the answer would be, so I let it go at that.

Anyhow, I really didn't have time to dawdle—for Arletta's good deed had stirred something within me, and now, pricked on by conscience as I hurried through the Quarter in the late afternoon heat, I was a man—a Best Man—on a mission. At the Metropole, when Bikey bowed me into the elevator, the lipstick imprint on my cheek, in conjunction with my disheveled suit, elicited another whistle, but I was so preoccupied that I forgot to tip him. I went straight to my room and sat down on my little bed and picked up the phone and called . . .

Not (perhaps to my eternal discredit) Betsy. But on the plus side of the ledger, in accordance with the Best Man Code of Honor, I did sit there and ring the emergency room of every hospital in the New Orleans phonebook, as well as two or three police precinct stations, the highway patrol, and (a late inspiration) the coroner's office, to inquire whether a one-armed guy from Oklahoma in a '54 Olds 88 had checked in. Had the rejected suitor attempted, in his despair, to end it all, or to drink his way out of the slough of despond? Apparently not; at any rate, no one-armed Oklahoman of record had been jailed or hurt or killed lately. After an hour on the phone, I could only conclude that by now Chick must be safely rolling along in the 88 on his way home to Arbuckle to await the coming of the Intershtate, driving one-handed, of course, and probably doing a pretty respectable job of it, since he didn't have the other hand to tipple with.

In any event, Best Man felt that he had done his duty, and deserved a little nap. So he stretched his heroic self out and took one, suit and all.

Well, from this point forward our story—okay, *my* story—will progress at a greatly accelerated pace. Indeed, except for a few loose ends, the story is over: Chick and Arletta and Fondelle and the evanescent Mary were, as we presciently say nowadays, history—along with the Reverend and Mrs. Hoakem, and Jay's unattainable sister, and Señorita Marta (though not her insidious little colony of illegal immigrants, who had yet to make their presence known), and all those other phantoms and phantasms who had populated what I supposed would be my last summer of single blessedness, the whole motley lot of them receding irretrievably into the past, going, going, gone.

Later that evening I ventured into the Quarter for one more shot at getting a little local color on me. I landed, eventually, at the Old Absinthe House itself, which, to my delight, was aswarm with the species boho — or, more probably, faux boho. I downed an untold number of Sazeracs, and in the process somehow fell among the poets, in whose company I regaled myself until, along about two in the morning, I noted with alarm a poetic hand upon my knee. I stole away and straggled back to the Metropole without incident — except that the oyster po'boy that had shadowed me all day finally mugged me in an alley off Dauphine, and pretty much finished off my seersucker suit.

From that night forward, by the way, I have struggled against the impulse to make a mental association between poets (absinthe guzzlers that they are, down to the lowliest versemonger) and oyster po'boys. And maybe I should also seize this opportunity to mention that it was to be many years before I would learn that the licorice in a Sazerac is mere flavoring; otherwise, oh my honeys, it's all rye whiskey and imagination, and not a drop of absinthe.

Nonetheless, I awoke the next morning with a Sazerac hangover the size of a Greek tragedy. I was, as we used to say of the hangovers of my youth, too sick to die. So, lacking that attractive option, I packed up, consigned my ruined suit to the trash, purchased Bikey's eternal loyalty with a farewell dollar bill (in penance for the deplorable condition in which I'd come in last night), and lugged my suitcase down to the Greyhound station. It had been my intention to take a bus out to the edge of town, where I planned to start hitching home to Maysville, the last leg of my great adventure. But so debilitating was my hangover, so sickly and dispirited had it rendered me, that when I crept up to the ticket window, I heard myself ask meekly for a one-way ticket to Maysville, Kentucky, please.

There ensued thirty-six sleepless hours of mobile misery, punctuated by brief interludes of bus station waiting rooms, bus station cafés, and bus station men's rooms—stationary misery, so to speak. That pernicious hangover—the nastiest and most tenacious I've experienced in sixty years of dedicated tippling—had taken possession of me for the entire duration of the trip, loyal as a succubus. Meanwhile, my nether person was more and more disturbed by those other little fellow travelers, who had at last begun to bestir themselves, and were soon gamboling about as if they owned the place.

During a 5 AM layover in Nashville, after my wee beasties had no doubt infested the latest of a dismal procession of Greyhound men's rooms, I went to the café for an ill-advised cup of Greyhound coffee, where I idly picked up a discarded newspaper and came across an item headlined "First Section of New Interstate Highway System Slated for Kansas." Poor Chick; he'd had a bad week. Perhaps it would've been some small consolation to him to know that his erstwhile best man was suffering too.

Yet, sick and exhausted though I was, scruffy, smelly, and (not that anyone would've noticed) unshaven, busted (after I'd paid for my bus ticket, Betsy's ring fund stood at twenty-seven lonesome dollars), brokenhearted (Ah, Fondelle! Ah, Mary!), beset by pubic grasshoppers (Ah, treacherous Marta!), despite all that, jouncing along hour after hour in that Greyhound meat wagon came to seem, amazingly, both a fitting conclusion to my summer of adventure and a quixotic fancy in its own right, a latter-day version of riding the rods, of becoming One with the Great Unwashed. And to be taking home with me, as souvenirs from exotic climes, not just a severe case of the galloping dandruff but what I firmly believed was a real, live absinthe hangover . . . Oh my, it was a dreadful trip; I wouldn't have missed it for the world.

These entertaining diversions notwithstanding, however, I found time along the way to make two firm promises to myself: First, I did not intend—not under no circumstances whatsoever—to marry Betsy. Second, no power on earth could keep me from going back to California. And may I precede myself just long enough to say that I kept both resolutions? (Which is how it came to pass that one year later almost to the day, still in a state of blessed singleness, I would be heading west again, this time in my Bel Air, bound for Stanford University, where I hoped to learn the tricks of the freelance writing trade.)

Any-hoo (Ah, Fondelle, Fondelle!), when the Greyhound paused briefly to drop off a passenger in Washington, Kentucky, a scant three miles south of Maysville, I was struck by a sudden inspiration. Leaping to my feet, I grabbed my suitcase from the overhead rack and got off too. As soon as the bus pulled away, I stuck out my thumb and, after a very few minutes, I caught a lift with an old guy in a pickup, who was hauling a big crate of live chickens to town. Perfect! He let me out ten minutes later in downtown Maysville, where, by another delicious stroke of luck, an old high school buddy happened along just in time to witness my arrival.

"Hey Eddie," he called, eyeballing the suitcase. "Where you been, dad?"

"California," I answered happily. "I just hitched in from the Coast."

ANOTHER GREAT MOMENT IN SPORTS

Eddie Clammerham, the Wayward Youth with the Tony Curtis forelock, is all grown up; he boasts a family, a ponytail, and a tenuous grip on a lectureship at Stanford University. And he has declared himself an implacable foe of the war in Vietnam, against which he is, on a certain brilliant Palo Alto spring morning in the late 1960s, smack in the midst of the most massive and potentially most volatile political demonstration ever launched here on the campus of his nominal employer, the Harvard of the West, where the ghost of Herbert Hoover, stern and dour, still stalks the ivied halls, looking like a cartoon of himself in a Democratic newspaper.

Okay, maybe not all that implacable. I was thirty-six years old, you understand; my forelock was already somewhat grizzled, and was beginning to resemble Everett Dirksen's more than Tony Curtis's; and I had five hungry mouths to feed, of which the largest, and perhaps the hungriest as well, was my own. And jobs at Stanford University—especially menial little part-time temporary numbers like the one I had been clinging to for years—were hard to come by, and easily lost; we untenured incendiaries skated on ice as thin as our political convictions.

The target of this particular demonstration was a small, nondescript building called "the Hanover Avenue Facility" of the Stanford Research Institute, a think tank that did a great deal of contract work for the Department of Defense and with which the university itself, under fire from antiwar zealots, had recently and rather sententiously severed its connection—at least to the less than excruciatingly painful extent of officially changing the institute's name to "SRI." Actually, all of the really important defense work was carried on at SRI's sprawling complex of offices in Menlo Park, a couple of miles from Stanford, but the organizers of the demonstration had chosen to hit the Hanover Avenue Facility because it happened to be conveniently situated just off the campus—reminiscent of the old joke about the drunk who lost a dime in a dark alley and then was seen searching for it under the streetlamp at the next corner, where the light was better.

The fact is, I didn't much want to be a party to this demonstration anyhow. In the first place, in order to throw our inconsequential bodies on the line and stop the Odious Machine, it was necessary that we gather in front of the Hanover Avenue Facility at the unseemly hour of 6 AM, so that we could liberate SRI's oppressed and benighted slave-laborers as they arrived for work. Now this is 6 AM in the *morning*, folks—a time of day when, according to my limited experience, the very air outdoors is fouled with noxious morning vapors, and sensible people are snug in their beds at home.

I'd been involved in all manner of rallies, sit-ins, teach-ins, and countercultural soirees, most of which had at least started off as very tame affairs; if they later grew a bit . . . raucous, it happened spontaneously, in response to the circumstances of the moment—as when, for instance, our estimable vice president Hubert Humphrey came to campus to deliver a speech defending the war and, with his sophistries and hypocrisies, turned an ill-disposed but perfectly peaceable audience into a raging, slavering mob that would have spanked him soundly and sent him to his room if it could've laid its collective mitts on the slippery old scamp.

Once upon a time, and not all that long ago either, there'd been something called the Peace Movement, comprised largely of softhearted, softheaded liberals not unlike myself—We Hapless Few, as it were. But now the Few had become Many, and the Peace Movement had become the Resistance, and at Stanford its leadership had devolved into the hands of the most bellicose, doctrinaire Richie Rich revolutionaries on campus, a sort of foreshortened Rainbow Coalition that arced all the way from the Red Guards to the White Panthers, with a bland, colorless mass of liberal softies in the middle, holding up the whole airy illusion like the meringue on a moose-poop pie.

So we are gathered, perhaps three hundred strong, just after sunup on the little crew-cut front lawn of the Hanover Avenue Facility, to receive our marching orders. Our leaders, in their undergraduate wisdom—egged on by a single Maoist English professor and a pack of hectoring grad students and junior faculty—have been defiantly bearding the local constabulary, via the media, on a daily basis, vilifying them as pusillanimous porcine poltroons and hinting darkly that they will be subjected to all manner of unspeakable indignities if they dare to interfere with our amiable pursuits—with the predictable result that behind one of the nearby buildings is a small army of angry cops in full riot gear, complete with rifles mounted with tear-gas grenades.

Not to worry, though, because each and every one of us devilishly cunning anarcho-syndicalists is (supposed to be) equipped with a trusty Wet-Hankie-in-a-Baggie Tear-Gas Neutralizer Kit. (Mine is in the hip pocket of my low-rider bell-bottoms; I'm crossing my fingers that it won't start seeping at some unseemly moment.) According to current counterculture folklore, a wet bandanna tied burglar-style about the lower face will turn away tear gas like a soft answer turneth away wrath—both very shaky propositions, as events will all too shortly demonstrate.

About a block from where we're now assembled, Hanover Avenue ends at Page Mill Road, a major traffic tributary, and half a block from there Page Mill meets El Camino Real, the principal business artery of the entire bayshore side of the San Francisco Peninsula; at the morning rush hour—coming right up—it's one of the busiest intersections in the area, and the perfect spot to administer a dose of urban grid-lock to the local body politic.

To that purpose, Our Leaderships are just now informing us, they have dispatched a small squad of Bolshevik grem-lins to prank with the morning traffic. (Sure enough, I can already hear from over at the intersection the plaintive beep-ing of the disgruntled early-bird commuter.) This tactic, we are assured, will distract the police and render them puny in the face of our righteous indignation, even as it secures forever our place in the minds and hearts of the People.

Beep, beep.

Actually, the troubling aspects of this demonstration ema-nated not so much from the leadership as from the follower-ship, of which I was a charter cipher. After all, we were supposedly smart folks, here at the Harvard of the West; if we were being led astray it was our own damn fault.

But for the last few months it had been just about impossible even to *identify* the leadership, never mind making an impression on it. Indeed, as best I could determine, there *was* no leadership. Oh, strings were being pulled behind the scenes, no doubt, and there were always plenty of officious types running around barking orders ("Awright, People! Go immediately to your Affinity Group!"), and no end of passionate—not to say loud—speechifying, theorizing, and philosophizing. Sometimes, at meetings and rallies, the air would fairly ring with the clangor of clashing dialectics.

And out of this unseemly discord would somehow emerge the policy du jour. For ours was what we proudly called a Participatory Democracy, which seemed to mean that tactical decisions were arrived at spontaneously, by unanimous impulse, with all the scatterbrained coherence of the flight pattern of a flock of grackles. Participatory it certainly was, but I have no idea why we called it a democracy; I don't recall ever once voting on anything, or even being asked for my opinion (although I meekly volunteered it now and then). Just showing up seemed to be all that was required.

Beep, beep, bee-e-e-eep!

Tresidder Student Union is situated near the center of the Stanford campus; its "front yard," so to speak, is White Plaza, an open space officially designated the campus Free Speech area. Tresidder even has a front porch of sorts, a broad, sun-struck stone patio with tables and chairs, a loafers' paradise where my friends and I used to drink coffee and talk politics till the very air turned pinko.

Meanwhile, if there was a rally going on out on White Plaza, the political invective would be flying as thick as Frisbees in the springtime, and when there was no rally in progress, the likelihood was that the male student firebrands would assemble on the plaza for the purpose of playing, of all things, football, that most philistine of undergraduate pursuits. They weren't going at it seriously, of course—just tossing the ball around. But there was an almost poignant irony in the very notion of these dedicated, passionate young un-Americans—not, in the context of the place and the times, a term of opprobrium but a badge of honor—engaging in this all-American pastime.

The irony did not, I think, escape its perpetrators. For the long-haired beardnik eggheads were actually pretty handy with the football—good enough, at any rate, to impress the passing Stanford coeds and make the frat boys recon-sider some of their fondest preconceptions. It was a dia-bolically subversive act, this frolicsome chucking about of the old pigskin, a cleverly disguised Bolshevik recruitment commercial.

Among the regulars was an undergraduate activist I'll call Norman, as unlikely a candidate for gridiron glory as you'll encounter anywhere. A declared Maoist with a minor in overthrowing the state, Norman was a tall, pallid, some-what overweight kid who looked as if he'd spent his entire life pearl-diving in the library. But there must've been a quarterback bottom-feeding in his gene pool, because he could indisputably throw the football—great, soaring, spiraling rainbow passes that found the intended receiver with uncanny accuracy.

Norman was equally prominent among our so-called leadership. He was a forceful speaker, he had dat ol' dialectic down pat, and he was brave; in each of the two sit-ins I'd been a party to, he was the first to enter the building and one of the last to leave. Somewhere I'd heard he was the scion of a Chicago family of working-class Jewish socialists, which alone would make him an anomaly in the Stanford WASPs' nest and probably go a long way toward explaining why, despite his pudgy, unprepossessing exterior, he seemed tougher than his movement peers, readier for action, more serious, and at the same time more exuberantly revolutionary. Unlike all too many of the rest of us, he wasn't rebelling *against* his heritage, he was rebelling *with* it.

Anyhow, on the morning of the Hanover Avenue Facility action, it's no surprise that Norman—looking rather dashing, actually, with his wet bandanna tied fetchingly around his forehead and, for some unfathomable reason (it's not a bit cold out here), a black leather glove on his right hand—is once again making his presence felt. Right now, he's standing atop the front steps of the building, speaking through a bullhorn, laying out for us the tactics the lead grackles recommend this morning. We are to divide ourselves, it seems, into two groups: the "peaceful protesters" will go across the street and trudge up and down the sidewalk carrying peace signs and singing "We Shall Overcome," while the "militant cadres" (the Maoist English professor is nowhere to be seen, but his language is still very much with us) will link arms in a human chain across the building's entrance, heroically interposing their own personal bodies between the SRI war machine's wretched wage slaves and their cruel masters. There is little question which group Norman intends to ally himself with.

For me, however, the decision's not quite so obvious—because, you see, there are all those cops. They've moved out into the open now; over my right shoulder I can see a noble phalanx of them formed up military-style on the greensward between our building and the next, maybe as many as a hundred cops all decked out in sidearms and bulletproof vests and those spooky helmets with the Plexiglas face masks, the front ranks bearing their grenade-launcher rifles at the ready, the rear guard wielding black nightsticks the size of a caveman's bludgeon.

Over my left shoulder, in the meantime, a monumental traffic jam has been a-building. Smack in the middle of it I can see the long yellow hump of a school bus, sitting crosswise in the intersection of Page Mill and El Camino.

Someone says that one of our gremlins crept up under its hood and made off with the distributor cap.

The din is tremendous: an angry cacophony of car horns, police sirens, and bullhorns. Over where the cops are gathered, the rising sun glints menacingly off all those face masks; the riflemen are doing some sort of thrust-and-parry drill with their grenade launchers, while the rest of the troops, rarin' to crack some Commie noggins, smack their palms impatiently with their giant nightsticks.

Now, I have the heart of a lion, as is well known in literary circles; nonetheless my feet, those shameless cowards, march straight across the street and fall in with the peaceful protesters, who are shuffling along like a chain gang, as if they've already been busted, beaten, jailed, and nominated for martyrdom. In my mortification, I humbly take up a sign emblazoned with the ubiquitous peace symbol—appropriately (in my case) nicknamed "Footprint of the American Chicken"—and begin slogging the line.

But after fifteen or twenty minutes, I know that if I have to mutter one more chorus of "We Shall Overcome," I'll be in danger of doing something awful that will bring down contumely and disapprobation upon the entire worldwide peace movement. Sincerity is a virtue, but these folks have OD'd on it; they should continue this march straight down El Camino to the local detox center. So I ask the guy in front of me—a divinity student, wouldn't you know?—to hold my peace sign for a minute, and head back across the street to jump-start the Revolution.

The police have cordoned off Hanover Avenue to automobile traffic, so the street teems with demonstrators. Norman has taken charge of the bullhorn again and is making what must be a terrific speech, judging from the number of "*Right on!*" points the crowd awards him every time he bellows, "ALL POWER TO THE PEOPLE!" There are a couple of TV news outfits on the scene, and flashbulbs are popping everywhere, like daytime fireflies.

The tension—like the racket—is almost palpable. The very air is thick with it; just crossing Hanover Avenue is like walking into a powerful psyche-sonic headwind. There's a line of cars stretching out of sight up Page Mill Road behind the campus, and the word is that traffic on El Camino is already backed up for miles, and right now every single one of those cars is blowing its infernal goddamn horn. I quite literally cannot hear myself think; I am giddy with fear, yet reckless abandon fills me like an inspiration. As I make my way through the crowd, I spot a guy I know, a poly-sci grad student named, let's say, Ronnie, in the human blockade. I break in next to him and lock arms against the boobarian hordes.

Ronnie, as it happens, is a fellow Southerner. Like me, he is strangely alight this morning with revolutionary zeal; his eyes are blazing unnaturally. He looks a little crazy.

"Ed McClackerty," he shouts above the din, "today I found out what I am!"

"Far out," I holler back. "What are you, Ronnie?"

"Ed McClackerty," he cries—and now he disengages his right arm to thrust his fist exultantly at the heavens—"*I'm a street-fightin' man!*"

"I like a man who knows what he is," I tell him politely. But the noise drowns me out.

Approaching us now is a nondescript little gray gent in a coat and tie—obviously an SRI lackey, poor devil—trying to go to work, he explains in a middle-European accent. No no, brother, we respond in several dozen voices, no work today, today we stop the war in Vietnam! I don't have nossing to do vith that, he protests, I study traffic patterns in Sunnyvale! Nonetheless, we turn him away, and as he goes off, grumbling, I ask Ronnie (at the top of my voice) how many other war criminals they've turned back this morning.

"Oh," he shouts cheerfully, "just him. He was the first one. The rest all went in the back door."

Say what? I glance behind me and, sure enough, there beyond the plate-glass doors are half a dozen SRI types— *inside* the building, mind you—standing around watching us as though we were already on the evening news. And then at that moment who walks up behind *them* but the little Sunnyvale guy we just turned away!

Slowly the scales fall from my eyes, and when they do the

first thing I see is that this human blockade is an absolute sham, and we're about to get our heads cracked open for the crime of . . . loitering.

Mumbling something (at the top of my voice) to the street-fightin' man about needing to take a leak, I pull out of the line and plunge back into the crowd, which has become even more restive; passing through it is like pushing through the directionless shove and tug of heavy surf. Bullhorns are blaring, but no one seems to be listening. A few people are hastily tying on their wet bandannas, but many more, having confronted the awesome reality of the juggernaut that's about to descend upon them, aren't even bothering. The rousing bravado of an hour ago has mostly vanished; suddenly everyone looks apprehensive, and there's a potent miasma of impending panic on the air.

Down at the end of the block, where Hanover meets Page Mill, some kind of rumble is in progress; over the heads of the crowd I can see revolving blue gumball-machine lights, and people are craning for a look. Behind me, a woman screams. I hear the muffled *whumpf* of what is, I will realize momentarily, the launching of the first tear-gas grenade. It lands on the street somewhere off to my right — *thwok* — at the fringes of the crowd. More screams, more *whumpfs*, more *thwoks*. My first thought is to seek what I imagine to be the relative safety of the peaceful protester ranks, but I reach the street in time to see those good souls disband in wild disarray, a hissing, fuming grenade having just landed *thwok* amidst them, like a missive from Old Man Hate himself. So much for the soft-answer defense.

The human blockade, meanwhile, has proved itself all too human; like the peaceful protester brigade, it has hastily disassembled itself and melted away into the milling crowds. Already a poisonous fog hangs over us; every stifling whiff of it is a malediction, a dire promise that something truly evil is about to happen. To my right, a chant goes up: "WALK, DON'T RUN! WALK, DON'T RUN!" Instantly, people start running; behind them, the police are on the move. For a long moment I stand there rooted in—again appropriately—the middle of the road, immobilized by uncertainty and fear, as the crowd surges around me, moving down Hanover in the direction of Page Mill.

"WALK, DON'T RUN! WALK, DON'T RUN!"

I try to obey, but once I finally start moving I find it utterly impossible not to run. As I yield to that imperative, I notice that the runner on my immediate right, maybe eight or ten feet away, is young Norman, he of the grenade-launcher throwing arm. He is still wearing his black glove, the mystery of which is about to be revealed to me.

For at that moment a tear-gas canister—they're about the size of a sixteen-ounce can of Colt .45—lands precisely between Norman and me; sizzling venomously with noxious gases, hot as a two-dollar pistol, it bounces on the pavement once, twice, then rolls to a stop as Norman catches up with it, reaches down, and scoops it up—with that gloved hand, of course—executes a full 360-degree spin without missing a beat or a step, and heaves the canister in a long, spiraling lateral trajectory straight through a big plate-glass picture window on the second floor of the Hanover Avenue Facility. In the final instant before grenade meets glass, the stricken face of a woman appears at the window, then vanishes as the missile punches through and a dense cloud of tear gas fills the room within.

So you might say that Norman has been preparing all his life for his Clear Moment, sacrificing hours of reading Marx in the library to work on his forward pass so that he'll be ready when the time comes, planning for that nanosecond in history that will mark the convergence of the hot grenade, the glove, and the plate-glass window. And when it arrives, there is only one thing to do, which he does; and only one way to do it: Perfectly. Which he does.

We're all in full retreat now, stampeding down Hanover with the canisters *thwok*ing here and there, hurrying us along. At the intersection, the convoy of patrol cars I'd noticed earlier has arranged itself so as to force us up Page Mill, away from El Camino; there are also a dozen or so cops lined up across the road, in full riot regalia, truncheons at the ready. As we round the turn, my recent acquaintance the divinity student, running flat-out like the rest of us but still doggedly carrying my peace-symbol-on-a-stick, cuts a little too close to the police line and instantly gets keelhauled and coldcocked for his audacity. The last I see of him, he's facedown on the pavement, one cop standing over him while another cuffs his hands behind his back. Beside him on the roadbed is the oversized footprint of the American chicken.

We have the right lane of Page Mill all to ourselves, but the left lane is bumper-to-bumper early-morning grumpy-to-start-with commuters who have been, thanks to us, immobilized for the last hour and fifteen minutes. Most of them appear to be reviling and defaming us behind their rolled-up windows as we mush along, gasping for a breath of air in the noisome fumes. Actually, though, their presence benefits us, inasmuch as the police, with all those witnesses on hand, are obliged to hold their wrath in check. They can't even drop more tear-gas grenades into our ranks, because if one of those big suckers went a little astray, it could put one helluva dent in the hood of some solid citizen's El Dorado.

The "Walk, don't run!" strategists are at our heels again, but this time we have the luxury of heeding their advice, because the cops are at *their* heels now, and the cops are walking too. Not at what you'd exactly call a leisurely pace, though; this is a forced march. They advance relentlessly, and we're still pickin 'em up and putting 'em down at a furious rate. Intuitively, I understand that if I were to stumble and fall, those walk-don't-run nags would walk right over me and leave me there like roadkill for the cops to work over and walk over in their turn, as they'd done so obligingly with the late divinity student.

("Late" doesn't mean the poor guy's dead, by the way; it just means I'd bet my ass he changes his major at the soonest opportunity.)

Off to our right, after we've progressed a few hundred yards up Page Mill, is a broad, open field of brown grass, and a handful of our number have peeled off from the Bataan death march and are over in the field calling and beckoning to the rest of us to follow them.

"No!" scream our self-appointed consciences, as in a single voice. "Stay together! Stay on the road! Walk, don't run!"

"Come with us!" cry the schismatics. "Come this way!"

For the third time this morning—the third time before breakfast!—I find myself on the horns of what is essentially the same dilemma, although this time it seems to have no moral dimension whatsoever: I simply have to decide—*right now*—whether my own best chance for survival is in numbers or in flight.

Flight wins! Suddenly I'm scrambling down into the little gully between the road and the field, on my way to freedom! Hey, that's it, I'll just keep on running, I'll run all the way to Canada! Unfortunately, however, I've forgotten all about the First Law of Revolutionary Physics, which is that tear gas is heavier than air. Stepping down into that little ravine is like plunging into the Love Canal: my own breath suffocates me, my eyes are blinded by my tears, I'm seismically disoriented, and I experience an attack of claustrophobia that would deck an exhibitionist. Weeping and gasping and choking and wheezing and reeling and lurching, I scramble out again, a far, far wiser man.

I am, I discover when I get my bearings, right back where I started—on Page Mill Road, surrounded by my chastened fellow insurrectionists. The difference is, they aren't going anywhere; the police have stopped advancing, and we, it seems, have retaliated by halting our retreat.

Let that be a lesson to them! All power to the People!

The demonstration was over. The cops stayed where they were until they got the traffic moving again, and then they allowed us to straggle back onto campus, a few at a time. There was a halfhearted attempt to rally our troops in White Plaza, but most of us just wanted to go to Tresidder and rinse the tear gas out of our eyes and sit down to a cup of coffee and a doughnut.

The revolution was over, too—at least as far as I was concerned. I was dog-tired, and I'd enjoyed all the amenities of it I could stand. I wasn't just temporarily tuckered out, either; this weariness ran deeper than that: it was positively existential. The time had come to tune out, turn in, and drop off. I would revolute no more forever.

Fast-forward now about twenty years, to the late eighties. I'm in the Atlanta airport, changing planes, when I notice this handsome, middle-aged young man in a pinstriped suit, Gucci loafers, and a belted raincoat, carrying a swanky leather briefcase and looking as significant as possible. It is, of all people, Ronnie, the street-fightin' man.

I identify myself, and he remembers me. We chat for a couple of minutes; then he glances at his Rolex and says he has to catch a plane. Well, I tell him as we part company, it was good to see you, Ronnie. Where you off to?

"D.C.," he says, turning to go. "I'm a lobbyist for R. J. Reynolds."

O the clear moment.

A FOREIGN CORRESPONDENCE

In the summer of 1984, temporarily flush from the sale of the movie rights to my (ahem) widely acclaimed novel, I treated myself, my wife, our two small children, and my seventeen-year-old daughter to six weeks in England. We stayed in an apartment in a converted World War I installation called Old Coastguards on Chesil Beach, near the village of Abbotsbury, in Dorset. On our first day there our landlord drove me into Dorchester, eight miles away, and I rented, for the duration of our stay, a spiffy little red VW Polo (or Golf, as it was called in the American edition). I rented the car at an establishment called, euphoniously, Loders

Motors, through an agent named MacIntyre, a tough, cocky, handsome little Scotsman whose brusque manner made it clear that he was used to getting his own way, by and large. Mr. MacIntyre insisted, in no uncertain terms, that I purchase accident insurance on the car, although it was (as Mr. MacIntyre himself readily acknowledged) painfully expensive.

I loved that little car. I had left my all-time favorite ride, a monstrous 1972 Plymouth Fury with a 360 engine and cruise control, huge and brown and ugly, big as an Essex yet sleek as a speedboat, back home in Kentucky, where it belonged. But the little Polo scooted around the skimpy Dorsetshire byways like a proper native of those parts, hewing stoutly to the left side of the road despite its driver's instinctive lurchings to starboard.

There were several other families, most of them English, who came and went during our stay at Old Coastguards, among them a tall, paunchy, young Manchester police officer I'm going to call Kenneth Widmerpool, and his wife and children. (And yes, I do admit that I purloined that name from a character in the novels of Anthony Powell, whose own Kenneth Widmerpool is quite possibly the most egregious ass in English literature since Bottom himself.) Now, as a thoroughly unreconstructed old hippie, I generally tend to eschew the society of policemen whenever possible, but this Widmerpool seemed amiable enough, and my kids and the little Widmerpuddles had hit it off rather nicely. So during the week they were there on holiday, the Widmerpools and my wife and I regularly enjoyed a little taste or three at the cocktail hour, sitting together on the terrace watching our mutual kids playing some unfathomable kid combination of kickball and soccer and dodgeball and croquet on the tiny Old Coastguards greensward below us, with the Channel, vast and gray-green and roily, in the background, Widmerpool and I enjoying each other's company almost as though we were soul mates, rather than, in real life, bitter adversaries.

So as I was backing the Polo out of the Old Coastguards driveway one evening late that week after a couple of cocktails with my excellent friend Widmerpool and I sort of, heh heh, dinged the fender of his Vauxhall—the Polo was unscathed—I wasn't really all that disturbed. After all, I figured, I've got insurance, the damage isn't much (a little dent, a scratch or two), the Vauxhall is pretty well shot anyhow, and Widmerpool and I are the best of chums, so what's to worry?

Officer Widmerpool didn't disappoint me. When I went back up onto the terrace and confessed my crime, he laughed the whole thing off, and didn't even bother to come down to inspect the damage. Never mind, old boy, sez he, chuckling, tomorrow me and you will take a spin up to Dorchester and show these small-town blokes how a real big-city copper takes charge of the situation. My wife and I had some other errands to attend to in Dorchester anyhow, so Widmerpool and I arranged to meet at Loders Motors the following afternoon, where we'd get an estimate and set this little matter to rights. I called Mr. MacIntyre the next morning to tell him what had happened, and made an appointment to come in that afternoon, with Widmerpool in tow, to see him.

I dropped off my family at the Dorchester Marks & Sparks, to do some shopping. When I arrived at Loders at the appointed hour, Widmerpool's Vauxhall was already in the garage, and Widmerpool himself was engaged in rather heated negotiations, not to say a shouting match, with the shop foreman. Apparently, the foreman had estimated the damage to the Vauxhall at about forty pounds, max, whereas Widmerpool was loudly demanding an estimate of at least five or six hundred. He was, in fact, in an absolute rage, storming up and down the shop floor waving his arms about and threatening to bring a large detachment of the Manchester constabulary down to Dorchester and put the entire staff of Loders Motors in irons and throw them into the Tower of London for the balance of their miserable lives. Or words to that effect. And the foreman, not to be outdone, was giving it back to Widmerpool for all he was worth, menacingly shaking a large crowbar at him and calling him a bloody fool and a "cheeky, overbearing bastard."

I, meanwhile, stood by, figuratively (and perhaps literally as well) wringing my hands, feeling horribly guilty about having set in motion this whole colossal ruckus with my tipsy incompetence behind the wheel, yet at the same time rather enjoying the fact that here we had a genuine, certified cop—a cop, mind you!—who was ostentatiously revealing himself to be not just an officious capital-P Pig (in the approved 1960s sense) but an everyday greedy, grasping one as well. For it was slowly dawning on me that Widmerpool had from the very first regarded my little mishap as a golden opportunity to enrich himself by browbeating, blustering, and otherwise throwing his considerable quasi-official Widmerpudlian bulk about on the assumption that he could bully a few small-town panel-beaters into bilking my insurer out of a few hundred quid. These ruminations allayed my guilt to a level I could live with.

By now the general commotion had caught the attention of the shop manager and any number of mechanics, lube and oil guys, mufflerologists, and other untidy personnel who had joined the foreman in angrily rejecting Widmerpool's strident efforts to assert his authority. All work had been suspended in the garage; those employees who weren't themselves actively participating in the debate had laid down (or, in a few cases, picked up) the various tools of their trade to devote their full attention to the proceedings; had they elected to attack en masse, my Widmerpool would have been rendered one more greasy spot on the floor of Loders Motors. As the fracas approached a crescendo, Widmerpool vociferously called for justice—and the manager called for Mr. MacIntyre.

Enter MacIntyre. Actually, he'd been there for a while,

standing just outside his office door with his arms crossed over his sturdy little tweed-jacketed chest, biding his time. But when the manager called his name, every eye in the establishment, including Widmerpool's and my own, turned toward him, and a dense, gravid silence descended upon the scene. No doubt about it, at Loders Motors Mr. MacIntyre was, as we're all so very fond of saying nowadays, Da Man.

MacIntyre didn't say a word. Glaring gimlet-eyed at Widmerpool, he very deliberately crooked a come-along gesture with his forefinger, then wheeled about and stalked into his office without looking back. Widmerpool obediently followed him, and I, not knowing what other course to take, did likewise, closing the door after me. MacIntyre was already seated behind his desk, elbows on the desktop, his hands clasped before him in the familiar church-and-steeple fashion. I took one of the two chairs facing the desk. Widmerpool, his face flushed with stifled outrage, remained standing. MacIntyre eyed him through the little steeple of his forefingers as though it were a gunsight.

"Now see here," Widmerpool began, quickly gathering steam as he rose to his previous level of volume and vehemence, "I'm an officer in the Manchester police force, I know my bloody rights! I was sitting on the terrace minding my own affairs when your client"—that would be me—"your client smashed his bloody Polo into my Vauxhall and damaged it to such an extent that . . . that . . ."

"Look, old cock," MacIntyre interrupted, in a voice as

cold as a Scottish mackerel, "you know what I would do if I were you? If I had the great misfortune of being you, I'd shut my fucking gob."

Widmerpool's jaw dropped. "But this man here, this client of yours, he smashed his . . ."

Suddenly, I was experiencing a resurgence of richly deserved guilt. "Yes, that's right," I admitted sheepishly, "I did hit his . . ."

MacIntyre shot me a glance that plainly said, *You shut your fucking gob as well.* Which I did, instanter.

Widmerpool tried another tack. "Now this won't do! I'm an officer in the Manchester police, and . . ." But MacIntyre wasn't having any.

"Don't you try to pull rank on me, mate," he said, "for I don't really give a shit. You're not in Manchester here. If you're in the market for a dust-up, that fellow out there with the crowbar will give you one, I promise you. What you'd better do, my lad, is take that bloody fucking Vauxhall back to Manchester, and put this matter in the hands of your insurer. They'll get in touch with us, and we'll work something out. In the meantime, what you want to do is shut your gob and get your great arse out of my garage."

That pretty much finished Widmerpool off. Pale as a boiled turnip, he sputtered something about how Loders Motors would be hearing soon from his attorney, and beat a hasty retreat from the scene of battle. I rose as if to follow him, but MacIntyre motioned me to stay put.

"When does that brute go back to Manchester?" he asked when Widmerpool was thoroughly off the premises.

As a matter of fact, I told him, I believe the Widmerpools are leaving tomorrow.

"Excellent," he said. "And there was no damage to the Polo?" I assured him that there wasn't a scratch on it. "Now what you must do, Mr. McClanahan," he continued, "is just stay out of that bugger's way till he's gone. By the time he gets his report filed and the paperwork goes through, you'll be back in America, safe and sound. But I can tell you this"—he leaned back in his chair and locked his hands behind his head after the manner of a man supremely satisfied with himself—"I can tell you that our good friend Constable Widmerpool will not be collecting one goddamn halfpenny for this unfortunate little speculation of his. Not from us, not from you, and not from his insurer either."

I so admired the way he said "hayp'ny"—my favorite Briticism—that for a moment I was speechless. "But I did hit his car," I said finally, "so don't you think I should . . ."

"I think you should keep your mouth shut. Don't tell him anything, don't volunteer anything, and for the love of God don't sign anything. Just stay out of his fucking way. I don't doubt there'll be a few letters flying back and forth over the Atlantic, but if you're back home in America, they needn't concern you."

Puzzled, I wondered aloud how MacIntyre could be so confident that Widmerpool's own insurer wouldn't pay up, but he just smiled enigmatically and said I should leave that to him, which, of course, I was glad enough to do. I said good-bye and went to pick up my family at Marks & Sparks. After I described for my wife the delightful little contretemps I had just enjoyed, we decided that the prudent course was to contrive to absent ourselves from Old Coastguards for the remainder of the day. There was an Alec Guinness festival playing at one of the cinemas in town, so we spent the rest of the afternoon doing a little local shopping and sightseeing, had dinner at our favorite Dorchester pub, and then took the kids to see *The Man in the White Suit*. By the time we got home, the Widmerpools were long abed, and when we arose the next morning, they were gone.

Four months later, back home in Kentucky, I received the following letter, under the logo of Network Insurance Services Limited, addressed to one "E Lanham":

Dear Sir,
We are writing you as Brokers for our mutual client, Loders Motors Dorchester Limited with regards to an accident which occurred on 23 July 1984 whilst you were driving their hire vehicle QJ 8906. We understand that you were involved with a collision with a parked vehicle owned by Mr K Widmerpool and we have now received correspondence from his Motor Insurers and Solicitors acting on his behalf relating to the above

accident. Unfortunately, we have been advised by our client that no damage was sustained to vehicle QJ 8906 and the accident had not been reported to them by yourself.

If we are to deal with this matter on your behalf, we must ask that the attached Motor Vehicle Accident Report Form is completed in full and returned to us without delay. We must advise, that unless we do receive this completed document we will not be in a position to act further on your behalf. We look forward to hearing from you by return.

Yours faithfully,

A D Matthews, Claims Supervisor

Intriguing as I found Mr. Matthews's apparent regret that vehicle QJ 8906 had sustained no damage, I was even more mystified by his assertion that "the accident had not been reported to them by yourself." But as I had no interest whatsoever in having Network Limited "act further" on my behalf, I consigned Mr. Matthews's communiqué to the dead-letter file, and figured that would surely be the last I'd hear of it.

Then, three months later, E Lanham received a second communication from Mr. Matthews:

Dear Sir,

We refer to our letter of 3 October, and unfortunately cannot trace having received your reply.

We enclose a copy of our letter together with another Motor Vehicle Accident Report Form and would ask that you give this matter your urgent attention.

In view of the delay that has already occurred in this matter, we would also appreciate an explanation from you.

We now await your further advices in due course.

Yours faithfully,

A D Matthews, Claims Supervisor

Now at last I was beginning to get a faint glimmer of understanding of what was going on here: For all his smug confidence that his official status, such as it was, made him the master of petty bureaucratic procedures, Widmerpool's rage had blinded him to the immediate necessity of filing an official accident report at Loders Motors—and Mr. MacIntyre certainly hadn't been inclined to remind him of the oversight. And since there had been no damage to Loders' hire vehicle QJ 8906, the entire episode had disappeared from the public record—which meant that there was, officially at any rate, no second party involved in the accident, which in turn meant that Widmerpool alone was responsible for the damage, and that therefore his insurance company was balking at paying for it, or perhaps threatening to raise his rates to an insupportable level. Either way, it would prove the worse for Widmerpool, which was fine and dandy with me.

But with the terrible Mr. MacIntyre many months and

three thousand miles behind me, I allowed myself also to take exception to the veiled threat in that line about "we would appreciate an explanation . . ."

Shut your fucking gob, Mr. A. D. Matthews, Claims Supervisor, thought I; I'm a citizen of Kentucky, US of A, and you can't lay a finger on me. And so, from that vantage point, having determined that it was high time I had a little fun out of Widmerpool & Company, I wrote the following response:

Dear Mr. A D Matthews, Claims Supervisor:
First I must tell you that I regarded your letter of October 13 as a minor annoyance, and accordingly chose to ignore it. Now, however, comes your second, a piece of damned impertinence which rouses me to wrathful indignation.

You are correct in your statement to the effect that on 23 July 1984, whilst driving Loders Motors' hire vehicle QJ 8906, I was involved in a minor accident with a vehicle owned by Mr. Kenneth Widmerpool, of Manchester. It is also correct (though not, as I deem it, unfortunate) that the Loders vehicle sustained no damage. It is, however, necessary for me to demur in the strongest possible terms from the peculiar assertion that I did not report the accident. Indeed, having reported it instantly to Mr. Widmerpool—and in light of the fact that Mr. Widmerpool is himself a policeman, it might also be said that I simultaneously reported it to the police as well—I went with Mr. Widmerpool the following day to the Loders establishment in Dorchester, where the (very slight) damage to Mr. Widmerpool's vehicle was examined by the shop foreman, with whom Mr. Widmerpool then engaged in a difference of opinion so violent in its language and so strident in its tone that I feel safe in assuring you that it made the occasion quite memorable to all who were present or within earshot of it, including, in addition to the aforementioned principals, any number of panel-beaters, mechanics, managers, assistant managers, salesmen, clerks, stenographers, janitors, and innocent bystanders and passersby. I should not want for witnesses, you may be sure of that. Mr. Widmerpool and I were at last requested to repair (no pun intended) to the office of Mr. MacIntyre, the Loders associate from whom I had originally hired vehicle QJ 8906, where Mr. Widmerpool continued to express his point of view with undiminished vigor, to such an extent that Mr. MacIntyre, after reminding him that Manchester policemen have no standing whatsoever in Dorchester, felt called upon to request—not to put too fine a point upon it—that he betake his great arse off the premises.

So don't you tell me, Mr. A D Matthews, Claims Supervisor, that I failed to report the accident to Loders. Indeed, I spent the better part of a monumentally unpleasant afternoon reporting it to them and, by extension, to half the sentient population of Dorchester as well.

As to my further advices, those would perhaps best be summed up by the suggestion that you and Mr. Widmerpool and Network Insurance Services Limited—whose insurance is so remarkably dear—go forth and commit an act of carnal knowledge upon your several selves.

Yours faithfully, E Lanham

I also had rather a good time filling out the accident report form ("Whilst reversing in the Old Coastguards driveway . . ."), which I submitted with my letter. In fact, I so much enjoyed the part of the form that asked me for a "sketch plan" of the accident that I couldn't resist making a copy of it before I mailed it off to England.

This concluded my correspondence with Mr. Matthews.

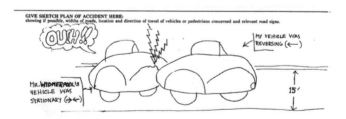

AND THEN I WROTE . . .

expect I might as well go ahead and own up, right off the bat, to the fact that this little morsel of writing has but one ambition, which is to provide a vehicle that will allow me, when my vast audience clamors for me to read my work in public, to inflict upon them—be warned—the only three songs I've ever written, rendered up, strictly Acapulco, in— be doubly warned—my very own inimitable singing voice.

(If you're so fortunate as to encounter these lyrics in some benighted region outside my vocal range, you'll have to invent your own tunes, which will almost certainly con- stitute an improvement on the original.)

That said, let's betake ourselves way up to the upper-left-hand corner of the country, where I am lumbering along a Montana freeway in a cumbersome, swaybacked old white whale of a '65 Chevy van named Moldy Dick, headed east, into the very first sunrise of July 1976. At my back is a U-Haul trailer and, receding into both the distance and the past, the town of Missoula, Montana, which until this morning I've called home for most of the past three years. Ahead of Moldy Dick and me is my new bride Cia, piloting our ageless VW microbus, the McClanavan, and ahead of her are a couple of thousand miles of eastbound highway, at the far end of which is a tumbledown four-room tenant house on a high bank above the Kentucky River, near the hamlet of Port Royal, in Henry County, Kentucky. In Moldy and the U-Haul are two-thirds of our worldly possessions; in the VW, with Cia, is the other third. Yet, as must ever be the case with nearly newlyweds, our hopes are high. We are nesters, homesteaders, a weird little wagon train in the Eastward Movement, pioneers seeking our earthly paradise.

Ten months earlier, Cia and I had set out from Missoula on the same highway, in the same direction, on what has to be one of the most feckless adventures in the history of human endeavor, a quest for—to borrow Tom Waits's title—the Heart of Saturday Night. Specifically, we were going to write a book about honky-tonks.

To that dubious purpose, over the next six months or so, honking and tonking relentlessly, we drove 14,000 miles, from

Montana to Louisiana to Kentucky and, by way of northern Mexico and Bakersfield and L.A., back to Montana . . . Like a lot of embryonic books, this one never happened, though I did get a chapter ("Drowning in the Land of Sky-Blue Waters") of my second book, *Famous People I Have Known*, out of it. *Famous People* is (also!) still available at fine booksellers everywhere, which is good, because it means I don't need to rehash here the intrepid details of our peregrinations; suffice it to say that we contracted a severe case of the honky-tonk blues, compounded by a touch of motion sickness.

Midway in our travels, Cia and I had taken a breather for a couple of months in that abandoned tenant house by the Kentucky River, on the farm belonging to my longtime friend Wendell Berry's uncle, Jim Perry, just down the road from Wendell and his wife Tanya's own farm, in the tiny community of Port Royal. In February, when we hit the road again on our return trek to Missoula, we already knew that we were coming back, and that our ultimate destination was right there at Uncle Jimmy's sweet little tenant house on the riverbank. We made it back to Missoula in time to fulfill our final obligations there—and now, three months later, in the early summer of 1976, we are setting forth once again, bound for Port Royal.

These old bangers of ours cruise at about forty-five, flat-out, which makes for a long, lazy day at the wheel. Ordinarily, lollygagging along all by myself like this, I'd pop the top of a cold Grain Belt, fire up a doob, and tune into the nearest call-in show on the radio. There are problems, though: For one thing, it's a little early in the day to dip into the mood enhancers; for another, Moldy Dick, which we bought for four hundred bucks just for this trip, came with a gaping hole, like a missing tooth, in the middle of the dash where the radio should have been. So, left to my own devices, too uncoordinated to twiddle my thumbs and steer at the same time, I'm casting about for something to occupy the vasty fastnesses of my mind for the next few hundred miles. And that's when I remember the Elbow Room, and the Born in the Land of Sky-Blue Waters sign.

The Elbow Room is a nondescript bar in a nondescript building which squats nondescriptly amid the used-car-lot ghetto on the south side of Missoula. It has a pool table, a good country jukebox, and a peremptorily amiable bartender, but by and large the atmosphere is pretty business-like, and the business at hand is alcohol. (A small sign taped to the backbar mirror discreetly advises that THE DOCTOR IS IN AT SICKS AM) The clientele is mostly trailer-court working class—day laborers and millhands and motel maids and Granny Goose salesmen and tire re-cappers and Korean War widows and Exxon pump jockeys—and it includes a sizable contingent of full-time, dedicated alcoholics.

Now, for all my inabstinent ways, I have never counted myself among that happy number, but when we lived in Missoula I did like to fall by the Elbow Room every now and then for a nightcap or three, just to clear my head after a hard day at the thesaurus or some trifling domestic impasse or a particularly egregious outrage on the evening news. The glum, podiatrist's-waiting-room anonymity of the place seemed to cool me out somehow, and many's the midnight hour I've whiled away sitting there nursing a shot of Brand-X bourbon and meditating upon the electric Hamm's Beer sign behind the bar, the one that bears the legend "Born in the Land of Sky-Blue Waters" beside an animated picture, which follows a rushing mountain stream down past a campsite with a red canoe, on down a riffle and over a waterfall and around an island and past a campsite with a red canoe and down a riffle and over a waterfall and around an island and past a campsite with a red canoe and down a riffle and . . . The Hamm's sign, with that mad little river rushing eternally up its own fundament, has always seemed to me an ineffably profound representation of spiritual isolation, a sort of horizontal electric mandala for contemplative drunks, and I have long aspired to write a country song about it.

Why not now? Sure! I'll call it "Drowning in the Land of Sky-Blue Waters"; it will be my personal anthem, an old honky-tonker's swansong. Within the next ten miles of freeway I've got the opening lines—"I've lost my way again / Out in this neon wilderness"—and something that passes, at least to my tin ear, for a rudimentary tune. By lunchtime I have the first verse all wrapped up, and by our afternoon beer break, somewhere in Wyoming, I've made it through the chorus. And before the sun goes down that evening, I am singing—if you can call it that—at the top of my inharmonious voice, the very first song I've ever written. No doubt there will be those who say that it should be the last as well, but that's *their* problem.

So, as Roy Rogers used to put it, "Now don't you worry, folks, we're a-gonna git them rustlers. But first, lemme sing ya a little song. It goes . . . kinda like this . . ."

Drowning in the Land of Sky-Blue Waters

I've lost my way again
Out in this neon wilderness,
Where the rivers run in circles
And the fish smoke cigarettes;

Where the only things that give me
Any peace of mind
Are a jukebox and a barstool
And a strange electric sign.

CHORUS:
'Cause I'm drowning in the land of sky-blue waters
Since I lost the way home to you.
Yes, I'm drowning in the land of sky-blue waters;
I need you to see me through.

I've seen that peaceful campsite
A hundred times tonight,
Where the campfire's always burning
And everything looks right.

But across that crazy river
In this godforsaken place,
A man is going under;
He could sink without a trace.

CHORUS:
For he's drowning . . . (etc.)

The Elbow Room is closing now,
And I must face the street,
Where the only rushing rivers
Are rivers of concrete.

There's no way I can cry for help;
My pride has got its rules.
But at last call for alcohol
My heart calls out to you:

CHORUS:
Oh, I'm drowning . . . etc.

Well, so much for my formative years in showbiz. My
marriage survived my singing—for a while—and we lived in

Uncle Jimmy's little house for the next four years, until our burgeoning family obliged us to seek more spacious accommodations. Our fortunes had improved by then to the point that we were able to buy a rickety but roomy old farmhouse up on the hill, a little closer to Greater Downtown Port Royal. I mention this otherwise irrelevant transition merely to demonstrate that at this stage in my life, I was interested a lot less in being a rolling stone and a lot more in becoming a moss-gathering, metaphor-mixing old stick-in-the-mud.

Yet my late-blooming homebody propensities hadn't quite overcome my still-urgent need to honky-tonk from time to time. And so, one Saturday night not long after my family and I had moved into our relatively stately new accommodations, I found occasion to sneak off down the road to Carrollton with a buddy of mine to our favorite local dive, the B&M Disco & Bait Shoppe, to tip a few cold ones. On the jukebox in the B&M was a song called, cross my heart, "You Fuckin' Jerk, You Piss Me Off," to which I, in my newly assumed role as a country squire and man of property, took umbrage.

So-o-o . . . I went home and wrote—yes, folks, that ominous premonition means you *do* feel a song comin' on—I went home and wrote the song which many critics, in their wisdom (though they could be wrong), have called my Greatest Hit. I'll explain in advance that Sweet Lucy is the consort of the equally unsavory Sneaky Pete who, the more observant of my readers may recall, abused me in my youth—and maybe I should also apologize for the fact that all two of my songs (so far) take place in joints (pun alert!) called the Elbow Room.

But what the hey, why should I? They're *my* songs, aren't they? So here, for your listening pleasure (or not), is

All the Roads in the World
(A Kentucky Derby Lullaby)

Rose came from Porter County,
Where she worked at Fruit of the Loom;
Hung out for a while down on Two Street,
In a place called the Elbow Room.

Took up with a trucker from Fargo,
Went out west for a while,
Danced topless in a bar in Chicago;
Came back showin' the miles.

CHORUS:
All the roads in the world lead to home, sweet home;
They all lead the other way, too.
Some have to go, and some have to stay;
And some are just passin' through.

Wayne was a drifter from Denver;
Blew in for the Derby, and stayed.
Took a job as a back-up bartender
The day of the Derby Parade.

Rosie was sippin' Sweet Lucy,
Watchin' the parade pass her by;
She stole Wayne's heart down on Two Street,
When he saw the tear in her eye.

CHORUS:
All the roads in the world . . . etc.

Wayne took out his pay in Sweet Lucy,
Right there at the scene of the crime;
Told his life story to Rosie,
And they danced till closing time.

They were lost till they found each other;
Tonight they know where they are.
For two rocky roads came together,
In a place called the Elbow Room Bar.

CHORUS:
All the roads in the world . . . etc.

Well, for the time being, that pretty much got the song-writing bug out of my system, an apparent miracle cure that was no doubt welcomed by my adoring public. But it turned out that the condition was chronic, and the long-dormant symptoms would return in 1986 to put me through one more little bout with the terrible reality that I can't sing a lick. (No, says my effervescent friend Paul Krassner, but you can lick a singer!) That fall, my (and Paul's) friend Ken Kesey called to say that he was about to publish his memoir, *Demon Box*. There would be a book tour, Ken said, and he was planning to take a break during his travels and come to Port Royal to visit us and the Berrys for a few days.

This was exciting news for my then-nine-year-old daughter Annie, who had never met Ken, but had heard Wendell and me talk about how much he loved kids, how entertaining he was with them, how he always had a ready assortment of magic tricks and songs and jokes and stories. For Annie, it was love even before first sight; she could hardly wait.

Okay, I told her, yielding to my old vice one more time; howzabout I write us a little song, and when Ken comes, you and I will sing it to him. So that's what we did; I wrote an itty-bitty ditty called "Jack the Bear" in honor of Ken's visit, Annie and I rehearsed it together for days, and when he arrived we sang it for him.

Ken professed to like the song, and of course he lived up to his billing—he always did—and Annie and her little brother Billy were enchanted by him. But after Ken resumed his book tour, Annie and I broke up our act—"Jack the Bear" being the only song in our repertoire—and Jack went into deep hibernation for the next decade and a half.

In 2003, two years after Ken's death, I edited the seventh and final issue of Ken's previously moribund old self-published literary magazine, *Spit in the Ocean*, and when Viking Penguin published *Spit 7* (subtitled "All About Kesey"), a band of a dozen or so superannuated but still serviceable surviving Pranksters, myself among them, put together a modest book tour for ourselves. We got Ken's famous bus, Furthur, out of mothballs and hit seven bookstore venues from Portland to Eugene to the Bay Area, doing readings from the book and skits about Ken, singing some of his favorite songs, and just generally paying tribute to his genius and his imperturbable spirit. We had a grand time and played to full houses at every stop, and I resolutely finished off my portion of each program by singing "Jack the Bear," once a welcoming greeting, now, sadly, a fond farewell.

Our final show was on a Saturday night at Moe's Books in Berkeley, where, by then, the lovely and talented Annie was a likely prospect (not to say a shoo-in) for a PhD in English literature at UC. And of course she was, by paternal injunction (and possibly even by choice as well) in our audience that evening, and of course I drafted her—paternal injunction again—to join me onstage for "Jack the Bear." Annie isn't nine years old anymore—indeed, she got a wolf-whistle when she came forward—but I assure you that, as far as I'm concerned, our Moe's Bookstore duet of "Jack the Bear" was, for me, the very best moment in the whole adventure.

The song, by the way, goes . . . sorta like this:

Jack the Bear
(for Ken)

He comes on like Jack the Bear;
He ain't no hippie and he ain't no square.

He's Jack the Bear of world renown;
He's Jack the Bear from out of town.

CHORUS:
Hey hey, Jack the Bear,
Hey hey Jack the Bear.

Jack the Bear is in cahoots
With big galoots in pinstriped suits.
Jack the Bear ain't got no roots
Except the ones inside his boots.

CHORUS:
Hey hey, Jack the Bear,
Hey hey, Jack the Bear.

Jack the Bear has heard the news;
He says that when you snooze you lose.
He says you reap just what you sow.
Now Jack the Bear has . . . gotta blow.

CHORUS:
Hey hey, Jack the Bear.
Hey hey, Jack the Bear.
Hey hey, Jack the Bear.
Hey hey, Jack the Bear.

DOG LOVES ELLIE

On Labor Day weekend of 1948, my parents and I moved from Brooksville, Kentucky, population seven hundred, twenty miles east to the Ohio River town of Maysville, population seven thousand. I had arrived at last in the Celestial City.

I was just a month shy of sixteen, an about-to-be sophomore at my new school, Maysville High. I stood six feet, two inches tall—a considerable height in them days, kids—and weighed 147 pounds; a year and a half ago, I'd been five-feet-five—and weighed 147 pounds. It was rumored, quite incorrectly, that I was gonna be a helluva basketball player. Secretly, I was afraid of my new height; it gave me vertigo.

During the first week of school, when I was also at the dizzying height of New Kid popularity, I made friends with a junior named Gene Manley, a jittery, bespectacled, round-chinned little guy whom I thought was just unutterably cool. Well, damn, he *was* unutterably cool; he played drums in the school band, he dated cheerleaders, and best of all, he drove this nifty little '32 Ford roadster, a mustard-yellow rag-top with painted-on crimson flames blazing back from the radiator, a rumble seat, foxtails, ah-oo-gah horn . . . a flivver straight out of *Archie and Jughead*. Talk about cool! On the Friday night of my very first week in Maysville, when I some-how insinuated myself into Gene's rumble seat—up front, riding shotgun, was an equally cool trumpet player named Johnny Gantley (think Ray Anthony! think *Young Man with a Horn!*)—I was, oh my, elevated beyond imagination.

Now I was already familiar with Maysville's many orna-mental features, and the one that had always most impressed me was the bridge, that lacy, graceful, mile-long silver arc with twin silver spires spanning the broad Ohio to the little community of Aberdeen, which, according to my informa-tion, consisted solely of roadhouses, beer joints, and similar wholesome attractions. Over the next few years, I would become as intimate with that bridge and the interesting diversions at its other end as I am, nowadays, with the route to my refrigerator. That first night, though, I knew only that every time Gene and Johnny and I putt-putted along East Third Street in Gene's flivver, past the sign pointing to Ohio, I experienced an unsettling little premonition that if I ever crossed that bridge for real, there might be no coming back.

Along about ten o'clock, on our umpty-umpth tour of East Third Street, we discovered that the entry to the bridge was blocked by a fire engine and two police cars—the entire fleet, basically, of Maysville's emergency response rolling stock—all with their spotlights trained on the near spire of the bridge.

What was going on, it turned out, had begun one night exactly a month ago, when a notorious Maysville bon vivant named Wild Bill Dugan had clambered drunkenly but intrepidly up—and up, and up—the swooping catwalk to the very peak of the spire, 150 vertiginous feet or so above the murky waters, before the cops and firemen hauled him down. They gave him thirty days for public drunkenness and disorderly conduct—and tonight, the minute they let him out, he had scurried straight back up, to finish off the remains of the fifth of gin he'd stashed up there . . . exactly one month ago.

But that was actually my second introduction to the high life that awaited me in cosmopolitan, metropolitan Maysville, home of the famous Browning Manufacturing Company—which was merely the World's Largest Pulley Factory, you understand—and the soon-to-be-famous

Rosemary Clooney and the already famous Maysville High basketball team, the Bulldogs.

Having started life in Brooksville, where hatred for Bulldogs was like mother's milk, I grew up a loyal Brooksville Polar Bear. (Hey, I made the junior high team! I averaged eight points . . . a season!) In small-town Kentucky in those years, high school basketball was assumed to be one of the pillars of Western Civilization—or perhaps it was the other way around. The Polar Bears came by their name honestly, the original Brooksville teams having played their first few seasons in an unheated tobacco warehouse. Later, in the early 1920s, the heyday of girls' basketball, my own mother and several of her sisters were star Polar Bears in Brooksville High's brand-new basketball palace, a modest little brick outbuilding with a playing court hardly bigger than a Ping-Pong table, the same gym I too would play in, utterly without distinction, twenty years hence. Girls' basketball, stifled by the imposition of a plethora of dispiriting rules intended to "effeminize" (or, if you prefer, "demasculinize") the sport, had by the 1940s been dropped by most Kentucky schools, including Brooksville High. Meanwhile, the boys' version of the game had become more popular than God, and the Polar Bears, despite their meager home-court circumstances, had an honorable—indeed a glorious—history: In 1939, led by Mooney and Marvin Cooper, top guns of the sixteen(!) fabled Cooper brothers, they won the state championship, a Cinderella accomplishment of

Hoosiers proportions; and subsequent Coopers and Cooper cousins beyond number — Earl, Clyde, Dale, John Foster, the Yelton boys, et al. — had kept the Polar Bears in contention in the Tenth Region ever since.

But Maysville strode the Tenth like a very Yao Ming throughout the 1940s, and the Bulldogs were in the state tournament almost every year; in 1947 they won it all, and in '48, just six months before we moved to town, they were runners-up. I, meanwhile, had largely been a plump, bespectacled little meatball plugging along in Brooksville, twenty miles down the road, striving with all my pudgy, ineffectual might to hang onto my seat at the far end of the junior high team bench — until, in the summer before my freshman year, the growth spurt struck me like Captain Marvel's transmogrifying bolt of lightning, and suddenly, unaccountably, I was looking down on people I'd long been in the habit of looking up to.

This flabbergasting development assured me of a spot in the junior high Polar Bears' starting lineup — I was, after all, the tallest kid on the team — but did little to enhance my skills: I started every game that season . . . and barely eked out my annual eight points.

The truth is, Brooksville was deeply conflicted about Maysville, which boasted, just a short Long Dog ride away, all too many of the amenities we rustics hardly dared to dream of, such as a public swimming pool worthy of Esther Williams and a dime store and the White Light nickel-burger stand and Schine's Russell Theatre (a gorgeous arabesque fantasy with a statuette of a seminude houri in the lobby) and Kilgus's Drugstore (where, if you were quick about it, you could sneak a peek at an astonishing little *Readers' Digest*–sized periodical called *Sexology*, in whose pages were displayed such pornopological images as a close-up photo of a certain primitive work of female body sculpting called the Hottentot Apron—an image so arresting that it vividly endures in my memory even now, six decades later). There was even, rumor had it, a real live two-dollar lady of the evening, if you knew how to find her. It was enough to turn many a Brooksville boy's head . . . and mine was already swiveling like a klieg light.

From the Brooksville point of view, Maysville would've been the fabled City on the Hill, were it not that, topographically speaking, it was the other way around. Brooksville stands at the highest point of ground in Bracken County— its courthouse clock and water tower (both of which I have scaled, by the way) are visible for miles around—whereas Maysville crawls along the banks of the Ohio, three miles long and only six streets deep. River Rats, we called 'em, masking our envy with disdain. In Brooksville, we knew for a fact that the wily Maysville coach Earle Jones, Evil Genius of the Hardwood, had snatched the great Kenny Reeves, one of the best players in the state during the mid-1940s, away from humble circumstances over in Ohio somewhere, and was paying him untold sums of money to play for Maysville, just so those mangy Bulldogs could routinely have their way with our Polar Bears three times a year.

For the 1947–48 season, my freshman year, Brooksville retaliated by importing a hulking, menacing center named Tony Maloney, a quasi-legal transplant from an upstate orphanage whose play was brutish enough to have left at least one opposing center in tears. (Tony's fate was to become the model for Monk McHorning, the title character of—you guessed it—that widely acclaimed novel *The Natural Man*.) But not even Tony could roll back the annual tide of humiliation; Maysville had dispatched us handily, as usual, in the regional, and then almost won the state championship for the second straight time.

Now my mom and dad were just as whacked out about basketball as everyone else was (and is) in our enlightened state, so every year they took me with them to Louisville for the Sweet Sixteen (as the state tournament was inevitably called), which meant that every year I was allowed, on the grounds of cultural enrichment, to cut three days of school and have my own room in the Brown Hotel and run around loose in downtown Louisville and watch a lot of great high school basketball. And every year the Bulldogs, having once again eliminated the hapless Polar Bears in the regional tournament, showed up in Louisville with the classiest teams and the most fetching cheerleaders in the Commonwealth—so that, over time, my favorite quadrupeds and secret heroes (don't breathe a word of this in Brooksville) had become not

Polar Bears but Bulldogs — Kenny Reeves and Buddy Gilvin and Buddy Shoemaker and Gus Stergeos and Elza Whalen and Emery Lacey and the Tolle brothers, Fats and Shotsie, and most of all, in the 1947 Sweet Sixteen, a pair of eighth-graders the sportswriters had nicknamed Dog and Como, who were just my age and were already, in my personal pantheon of demigods, international celebrities.

So Labor Day of 1948, the day my folks and I moved to Maysville, was a watershed in my life. That very day I changed my name, for ever and ever, from "Sonny," the diminutive cognomen by which I'd been known (if at all) in Brooksville, to the relatively Brobdingnagian "Eddie," as befitted my new height; and that very evening a nice old lady of our acquaintance fixed Tall Eddie up with Carla Browning, of the Browning Pulley Works Brownings, and Carla and I went to a movie at the Russell Theatre and then to Kilgus's Drugstore for Cokes, and right there on Kilgus's corner, Carla introduced me to . . . omigawd, it's . . . Dog and Como!

My apostasy was complete. Go Bulldogs!

A few months earlier I couldn't have dreamed that these two paladins of the hardwood (I myself was an aspiring sportswriter, and that sort of language was my soul's own music) would soon become not just my classmates but also my running mates and even, for one brief, inglorious season, my teammates, fellow Bulldogs.

Como was a handsome guy — some imaginative scribe

had fancied, not unreasonably, that his profile resembled that of the redoubtable crooner Perry Como—a fiery, red-faced demon on the basketball court but off it, as sweet—and about as thick—as a Kilgus chocolate malt.

Dog, on the other hand, was significantly less handsome but appealing nonetheless, a stocky, eager little ball handler and ball hawk—the sports pages had dubbed him "Bull-dog" not because they identified him with the team but just for his relentless tenacity on the floor—with deep, fawning brown eyes resembling a beagle's more than a bulldog's and an earnest, almost imploring manner that made him hard to resist when he asked you for "butts" on your current cigarette (meaning he got to smoke the last half of it) or wanted to copy your math homework or mooch a dime for the pinball machine at the White Light or even, on the basketball court, any time you had the ball and he didn't, a circumstance likely to reverse itself in your next heartbeat. When he turned those great, pleading brown eyes on you, he could steal the ball or your smoke or your homework or your dime—or, as I would find out all too soon, your heart's delight—with no more conscience than a stockbroker.

I believe I mentioned, a few pages back, something about my familiarity with the ornamental features of Maysville, and how the bridge to Aberdeen was my favorite—but that was before I'd seen Ellie Chadwick.

Ellie was—and she remains—the loveliest fifteen-year-old who's ever bedazzled my unworthy eyes. (I exclude from this equation, of course, my own three lovely daughters, each of whom was once fifteen.) Inside my head I've been humming wordless paeans to Elinora Chadwick's beauty for almost sixty years, but now that I'm obliged, at last, to attempt an actual description of her, words fail me, and I find myself grasping at the stalest of clichés: flaxen hair shimmering like a sunstruck field of . . . well, damn, of flax, I guess; eyes as blue as cornflowers; a peaches-and-cream complexion; a smile to rival the lights of Broadway; a lilting voice; a figure wonderfully, sumptuously voluptuous yet at the same time as lissome as a willow switch; a girl fairly born to drive schoolboys to distraction, to inhabit their dreams both waking and sleeping, as though she'd been atomized and then dispersed all at once like a swarm of tiny Tinkerbells into the fevered imaginations of a multitude of Maysville's Lost Boys. So it was comforting—sort of—to know that at least I had company, plenty of it, legions of hopeless juvenile devotees just like me, all worshipping at the same shrine.

There was, however, one brief moment when I was *not* among that wretched number, one mortal instant in the measureless history of love when I alone of all the others stood before Ellie beneath a harvest moon and placed my trembling hands upon her perfect cashmere-sweatered shoulders and gently drew her to me and . . .

But I precede myself (a special talent of mine, as you may have noticed). Like every other schoolboy in Maysville, I fell for Ellie on sight, in my case in Miss Wallingford's English class on the first morning of school in the fall of '48, only twelve hours or so after Carla Browning had introduced me to Dog and Como. Carla, a very pretty girl who, unfortunately for whatever dreams I might have harbored overnight of becoming the premier tycoon of the pulley empire, went off to some fancy girls' school somewhere the very next morning after our bogus date and basically disappeared from my life forever. But Carla was no sooner beyond the city limits on that memorable morning when, downtown at MHS, just as the late bell began to jangle, the door to Miss Wallingford's ten o'clock English class opened and into my life stepped — be still, my heart! — Ellie Chadwick!

All that semester in English class, she sat in the row to the left of mine, one seat ahead, so that for fifty minutes every morning her immaculate profile was before me, a lovely, enigmatic ivory cameo. In homage to its alabaster perfection, I taught myself to write "Ellie" in the margins of my grammar workbook (the ever-popular *Keys to Good Language*) in fat, overlapping letters resembling nothing so much as a handful of amorous caterpillars at the height of the mating season, thus:

Still, smitten and stricken beyond salvation though I inconsolably was, during those first few weeks at Maysville High I became, as a Bulldog of far greater repute in prospect than I would ever be in retrospect, the Wild Bill Dugan of MHS society, scaling hitherto-unimagined heights of popular regard. Which brings us—almost—to that tremendous moment beneath that tremendous harvest moon. But first, a little scene-setting:

From the time I was old enough to pay attention to the funny papers, my favorite had been the strip called "Li'l Abner," by Al Capp. Abner, as everyone of my dwindling generation will recall, was a strapping, handsome young hillbilly, sweet but none too bright (not unlike my new friend Como), as evidenced by the fact that he preferred, unaccountably, the company of his pet pig Salome to that of his girlfriend Daisy Mae, a scantily clad, impossibly curvaceous cartoon rendition of . . . Ellie Chadwick! It was true! Daisy Mae really did look just like Ellie!

Okay, right, I need to take a deep breath here. But Daisy Mae *was* a dish, just as Abner was a dope, and therefore every year she pursued him, relentlessly but fruitlessly, in the annual autumnal Sadie Hawkins Day chase, wherein if a gal caught a fella, he had to marry her. And so popular was the strip that every autumn, on a certain Friday evening in practically every high school gymnasium throughout the land, there would be a Sadie Hawkins Day girl-take-boy dance, the only event of the year when the ladies were afforded the opportunity to select their escorts. And one morning in the autumn of 1948, only a couple of weeks before fall basketball practice would be exposing me (I didn't exactly know this yet, but I deeply feared it) for the fraud that I certainly was, who do you think Ellie Chadwick invited to the Sadie Hawkins Day Dance? Not Li'l Abner, not Dog or even Como, but Tall Eddie Clammerham, the Future of the Bulldogs!

It was, I think, the closest brush I've ever had with immortality. I was just arriving at the door of Miss Wallingford's English class when Ellie approached me, her books clutched to her bosom in the protective manner favored by schoolgirls in those pre-backpack days, and looked up at me with those dazzling blue eyes and smiled her dazzling smile and asked, so sweetly that I could almost feel my blood sugar level soar, if she could take me to the dance next week.

Take me? cried my inner juvenile delinquent. *O god yes, take me anywhere, and use me horribly!* Meanwhile, my candy-assed outer postadolescent, his knees knocking like castanets as he shuffled his great cumbrous feet somewhere way down there at the bottom of his interminable legs, stammered, "Um, um, um . . ."

Somehow, we arranged it: I would be Ellie Chadwick's date for the Sadie Hawkins Day Dance. Within the closely guarded ranks of postadolescent boys in those days—and doubtless in these days as well—it was the practice to trumpet one's conquests to the heavens ("I got bare braw!"

an erstwhile Polar Bear teammate of mine had once pro-
claimed ecstatically after an away-game ride home on the
team bus, with the cheerleaders aboard), yet as best as I
could determine by discreetly inquiring amongst my peers,
Ellie had never yielded so much as the first kiss. Indeed, it
was said that, due to her conservative parents' restrictions,
she'd never even had a date! To borrow Li'l Abner's favorite
exultation, O happy day!

There was, however, one small problem: I couldn't
dance. In Brooksville, girls would sometimes dance with
each other, but—perhaps for that very reason—Brooksville
boys generally ranked the terpsichorean arts somewhere
down around needlepoint. Whereas in Maysville, many of
my new friends, boys and girls alike, had matriculated at
Mrs. Brown's School of the Dance when they were in the
sixth or seventh grade, and by the time they got to high
school they had all the moves down cold, and could dip
and twirl like Fred and Ginger and jitterbug like Archie
and Veronica. Making matters worse, those who hadn't
gone to Mrs. Brown's had learned from those who had, so
that every kid in Maysville would be dancing circles around
the Bracken County bumpkin, laughing and pointing and
belittling—the latter being, I feared, the aspersion of choice.
My new manhood, my vaunted Eddie-ness, would be puck-
ered to the merest trifle before I'd danced a single step.

During those first few weeks of school, I'd made friends
with a junior named Darrell Henson, who owned a huge,

boxy, Capone-era Hudson sedan that some dead uncle had left him, and who was dating another of my pretty class-mates, Lucia Traxel, who happened to live in my neighbor-hood. So I proposed to Darrell that we double-date for the Sadie Hawkins Day ordeal, and to Lucia that she undertake, in the scant seven days remaining to us, to teach me how to tango.

Or at any rate how to do the box-step, which, despite dear Lucia's best efforts, proved to be the very maximum that she could accomplish in those seven desperate eve-nings of stumbling about with me in the Traxel family's basement rec room to the dreamy airs of Guy Lumbago and His Royal Pains issuing from an ancient windup Victrola. As its name suggests, the box-step—one step forward, one step right, one step back, one step left, one step forward—is a stiff, plodding, robotic sort of business, the ballroom equiva-lent to marching in place, performed largely in disregard or defiance of whatever music actually happens to be playing at the moment. If that lonely old blind man who taught Dr. Frankenstein's creation how to smoke had also under-taken to teach the monster how to dance, rest assured they would've done the box-step.

It probably didn't help that, on the eve of Sadie Hawkins Day, I had used my sixteenth-birthday money to buy myself what I'd imagined would be the coolest footwear on the dance floor, a pair of blue suede Thom McAns with two-inch-thick crepe soles, cosmic clodhoppers that weighed about eight pounds apiece and rendered me even taller and gawkier than I'd been in my old penny loafers, and my lumbering box-step even clumsier and more Frankenstinian than it had been in Lucia Traxel's basement. The music, once again, was recorded; I seem to recall that the first number was "A Slow Boat to China," and being torn between the dreamy escapism of the song ("I'd love to get you . . . on a slow boat to China . . . all to myself, a-lo-o-o-one") and the more immediate exigency of somehow escaping the agonies of the moment at hand. Ellie was as supple and lissome and light on her feet as a forest nymph, but I was steering her on a herky-jerky forced march to nowhere, and as we lurched about inside our invisible little box, I could detect, through the agency of the hand that now rested ever-so-tentatively at the (sigh) small of her back, a tiny, involuntary wince—call it a shudder—at every misstep (and there were many) of those monstrous blue suede concrete blocks I was wearing. The slow boat to China hadn't even left the harbor, yet already it was sinking like a stone, and its cabin boy—that kid with the concrete feet—was well on his way to becoming a hat rack for the fishes.

They must've played a couple more slow numbers in the early going, but hey, I was *dancing*, folks, I didn't have *time* to listen to music! I had been given to understand, I guess from movie musicals, that I was expected to initiate bright, scintillating conversation as we danced, but I was dumbstruck. Incapable of thinking and talking and dancing all at the same time—multitasking, we'd call it nowadays—I mindlessly, mutely propelled poor Ellie from invisible pillar to invisible post as, suffering like a *penitente* and sweating like a stevedore, I trod on her no doubt lovely little toes as though I were stomping slugs in the garden—or the graveyard—of my hopes and dreams.

That unhappy phase of my extremity ended—and another began—when someone put Glenn Miller's "Chattanooga Choo-Choo" on the turntable, which of course required one—or, rather, two—to jitterbug, and in turn required me to confess to Ellie, shamefacedly, that jitterbugging was utterly beyond my powers. I got through that mortification somehow, but as I steered Ellie toward the bleachers to sit this one out, who should pop up before us but that devilishly cool rascal Gene Manley, eager to boogie. Ellie graced me with a quick, apologetic smile, and then the choo-choo jitterbugged on down the line and left me standing in the station with the other wallflowers, in a sort of penumbra of commingled regret and relief.

Gene, who was such a tightly wound little bundle of nervous energy that he had no patience for slow dancing, delivered Ellie back to me when "Chattanooga Choo-Choo" gave way to some less vigorous tune, but we had barely made it back onto the dance floor when Johnny Gantley tapped me on the shoulder, cutting in. Johnny clung to the advantage for a couple of numbers until I. Jay Weaver, a smooth-talking senior, cut in on him, and then the ever-dangerous

Como cut in on I. Jay, and then I myself, Eddie the Unready, swung boldly into action and cut in on Como, but before Ellie and I had managed even one full turn around the narrow confines of the little rectangular plot of hardwood I'd staked out, Dog—him and his big, beseeching brown eyes and his ingratiating goddamn ways—he cut in on me, that dirty Dog, and away they waltzed!

Well, it was that kind of evening. The enemy was legion, and He was everywhere, in the persons of Gene and Johnny and I. Jay and Como and most of all the omnipresent, indefatigable Dog. There were, of course, a host of other interlopers as well, but none with so much staying power, such aggravating perseverance, such . . . dare I say it? . . . such sheer doggone *doggedness*. By eleven o'clock, when whoever was "spinning the platters" (an infelicitous locution which I sincerely hope turned into library paste in the mouth of the very first deejay who ever uttered it) signaled that the dance was over by putting Ray Noble's oleaginous "Good Night, Sweetheart" on the turntable, Dog had danced with Ellie about twice as many times as I had. Indeed, in order to dance the last dance with my own date, I had to cut in on *him*—and as he reluctantly released her to my custody (temporarily, as it turned out), he turned those great beseeching eyes on *me* . . . and hit me for a cigarette!

I'm pretty sure that after the dance, Darrell and Lucia and Ellie and I would've piled into Darrell's giant Hudson shoebox (a few months later, Darrell would put that old Hudson right through the front wall of some poor citizen's living room) and mo-gated up East Second Street to the East End Café for carbonated aperitifs, and logistics would've dictated that we take Ellie home first. Most of that has drifted away, though, into the mists of teenage history. But I do recall, luminously, that when Ellie and I arrived at her front door, that luminous harvest moon was looking down, and Ellie's luminously lovely face was looking up, and . . .

I'm tempted to describe our kiss as having been as tender and delicate and fleeting as a butterfly taking sweetness from a flower, except that I was certainly no butterfly. Nonetheless, with uncharacteristic courage, I wordlessly claimed the kiss and, to my astonishment, was granted it. Afterward, butterfly-like for once in my life despite that deadweight ballast of blue suede brogans, I floated off Ellie's front porch and back to Darrell's car in a perfect transport of delight. I could've plucked that harvest moon from the sky and put it in my pocket for a keepsake.

The next day, a Saturday, I was still all a-flutter, until I was brought crashing back to earth when I called Ellie and asked if I could take her to the Sunday-night movies at the Russell, and she apologized (not very sincerely, I must say, although she tried to be kind) for the fact that she already had a date: Dog, of course. I didn't even need to ask; I knew when I was whupped.

From that Sunday evening forward for the next three years, Ellie and Dog were as one, and to my knowledge Ellie never strayed. True love was true love, after all, and the Maysville High ladies generally kept things strictly on the up-and-up, and did but rarely go a-roaming. They were, by and large, Nice Girls, and in those days Nice Girls just didn't do that sort of thing. Despite that one delicious, indelible kiss, Ellie Chadwick, a very nice girl if ever there was one, would be, alas, forever out of reach, at least for me.

Dog, on the other hand, ran with the pack (of which I was a panting, slavering member), and on many an evening, after we had taken whatever minimal liberties were allowed us by the Nice Girls and had (metaphorically) put those vestal virgins to bed, we—the pack—were ourselves at liberty to go on the prowl, perpetrating all manner of after-hours outrages and indignities upon the public weal. Lured by those beckoning beer-joint signs, neon lodestars in the night, we crossed that stupendous bridge to Aberdeen and found our way to the Pennington Club and the Terrace Club and Danny Boone's Tavern and the Hi-Hat, and discovered that, as far as Buckeye bartenders were concerned, we were all absolutely eighteen years old, and legally entitled to drink all the three-point-two beer we required. After last call for alcohol at those accommodating venues, we were as likely as not to arrive, eventually, back in Maysville at the address of that even more accommodating—and even less discriminating—two-dollar lady down on Front Street. More often than not, Dog was an enthusiastic party to these revels, while Ellie, all unknowing, slept the untroubled sleep of the innocent.

———

Thus it came to pass that, heartbroken and forsook, I comforted my wounded teenage person during my high school years with tobacco, beer, pool, and all the complementary debauchery I could get away with—not much—during double dates at the drive-in theater, and all the commercial debauchery I could afford—which, after I'd budgeted for beer and smokes and pool, didn't amount to much either. My height, meanwhile, secured me one last eight-point season, this time as an apprentice Bulldog at the far end of the JV bench, after which Coach Jones reminded me that height wasn't everything, and suggested that I look into some other extracurricular activity, glee club or debate or something along those lines.

Ellie Chadwick was a varsity cheerleader by then, but— alas, alas—she would never cheer for me. All hope must be abandoned; it was probably just as well that I'd already gone ahead and consigned my soul to the devil anyhow.

To finance my expensive new appetites, I spent most of the summer of 1949 in a tobacco patch up on the hill above town, a long, narrow, mercilessly sun-baked strip of worn-out, yellow hardpan along the backbone of a ridge, chopping out weeds with a garden hoe at fifty cents per interminable row of stunted tobacco plants, which broke down to four dollars a day. I knew the story of Sisyphus and the great stone, and was frequently reminded of it during my own grim labors, by the way the weeds seemed to spring back up out of the ground almost as soon as I smote them down. But not even Sisyphus had to confront sweat bees and deerflies, armed only with a garden hoe, for four dollars a day. It was time to reconsider my career options.

That fall I accepted an after-school position presiding over the soda fountain at Kilgus's, pulling down a cool forty-five cents an hour. (The post, it seemed to me, wanted a dash of flash, so I taught myself to scoop one of those bulbous little five-cent fountain Coke glasses down into the shaved-ice bin, flip it end-over-end into the air without losing a single shaving, and catch it one-handed under the syrup spigot with the other hand already on the handle, ready to dispense a dash of the black, unpromising sludge that was the foundation of a fountain Coke.) And there were other compensations for working at Kilgus's: milkshakes to be guzzled and cigarettes to be pilfered and copies of *Sexology* to be spirited away and perused in the privacy of one's own . . . privacy. Girls came and went in Kilgus's in bewitching profusion from the minute school was out till closing time at nine (a few of them, I'm happy to report, specifically to marvel at my artistry with those Coke glasses), and the street corner right outside the drugstore was where I and all my friends hung out after-hours, loafing and smoking and trading dirty jokes and trying to cadge rides to the bright lights of Aberdeen. Kilgus's corner was, in fact, the very crossroads of Western Civilization . . . and don't think we didn't know it.

Ellie, like most of the high school girls, wasn't allowed to date on school nights, so Dog was usually prominent among us. Como, on the other hand, rarely showed up on Kilgus's Corner; rumor had it that he had taken up with the amorous, buxom, forty-something wife of a local grocer, and had but little time for boyish pursuits.

(Como's exertions in the backseat of the unwary grocer's car hadn't rendered him any sharper, though. Once, when he was a guest on Coach Jones's sports-talk show on WFTM, the local radio station, Coach asked him how many points he'd racked up so far that season. "Gee, I don't know, Coach," Como answered modestly. "About, oh, two hundred and thirty-four.")

After I hired on at Kilgus's, I worked evenings during the summer in the drugstore and supplemented my income with daytime jobs in construction as a hod carrier and pick-and-shovel guy. On Sunday afternoons in the wintertime I even served a stint as a cub reporter for the Maysville *Daily Independent*—or, as one of my wise-guy fellow knights of the plume liked to call it, the *Daily Disappointment*—writing obituaries for the Monday edition, an apprenticeship from which I received numerous early and unsettling intimations of mortality.

The Bulldogs continued to prosper as a Tenth Region powerhouse, although during my tenure at Maysville High they never quite made it back to the Sweet Sixteen. Como, nonetheless, played inspired basketball, and made the all-state list every year; when we graduated in '51, he was offered a full-ride scholarship by the fabled University of

Kentucky Wildcats. Dog also played brilliantly but always in Como's shadow, and by college basketball standards he was, as the unkind old joke has it, "short . . . but slow." No scholarship materialized, and as soon as Ellie left for the exclusive Southern college she'd long since planned to attend, he would be enlisting in the Air Force. Her family left town soon thereafter, so she rarely—if ever—came back to Maysville during her college years. To my knowledge, she and Dog never had another date.

As for me, I too matriculated at a snooty Southern college, which I loathed, and then transferred, as a sophomore, to Miami of Ohio, where I changed my name again, this time from "Eddie" to "Ed," having discovered that it was my fate to become, or rather to try to become, a writer, and calculated, no doubt mistakenly, that I'd be taken more seriously if I dropped the diminutive form. In pursuit of my muse, I eventually went west and spent most of the next twenty years writing and teaching at universities in Oregon, California, and Montana, then landed, broke and jobless, back in Kentucky in the late 1970s, this time to stay. In effect, I had recrossed the bridge at last, very much the worse for the twenty years of wear and tear, and very glad I was to be back home again.

Como starred on the Wildcats' freshman team, but his GPA was about as robust as my old eight-points-per-season scoring average, and, as all who knew him could have predicted, he flunked out after one season. A pretty good high school baseball player, he then tried out with the Pittsburgh Pirates, who gave him a $500 bonus and signed him to a minor-league contract. They sent him to play outfield for a Class-D team somewhere in the Midwest, but he "threw his arm away"—his term—making an ill-advised long throw to the plate in his very first game, and was home within a week. I never saw him again after that summer, and I don't know what he did with the balance of his life, but I do know that when he was in his late fifties or early sixties he got gut-shot by a woman—another predictable development—and died after months in the hospital. A friend told me that she went to see him during his final days, and that he was as handsome and sweet and sunny as ever.

The Air Force sent Dog to Japan during the occupation, and I lost track of him for quite a while. After his tour in Japan was over, he made his way down south, went into business (snack foods distribution), married, had kids (including a daughter named, I heard, Elinora), divorced, remarried, and perhaps divorced and remarried again. In later years, whenever I came home to Kentucky to visit family and friends, I heard reports that Dog—who came home periodically for the same reasons—had never gotten over it, that the old torch was still burning bright, that he still carried Ellie's senior photo in his wallet. (I knew that photo well, having carried its duplicate in my own wallet throughout my undergraduate years.) According to one of the more romantic versions of the story, he'd even engaged a Tokyo street artist to do her portrait, taken from the same photo, and had cherished and venerated it ever since. I envisioned Ellie's portrait, flanked by the matched pair of gleaming, gold-plated All-Tournament trophies Dog had won in the Sweet Sixteen in 1947 and '48, displayed in some sacred niche or grotto somewhere deep in the interior of every life he'd ever lived.

But for most of her admirers, the Ellie pipe dream went up in smoke when, after college, she married a no-doubt handsome young fellow from up east—I'm guessing he was a lawyer—went with him to New England, had a family, eventually divorced, and never remarried.

So tempus fugited apace, and the next time I looked up, forty years had passed, and suddenly it was the spring of 1991, which would mark the fortieth anniversary of my high school graduation. As it happened, Maysville High was being gobbled up by a gargantuan new consolidated county school, and would be closing its doors forever that same spring. Plans were afoot for a grand all-day reunion of MHS alums on the first Saturday of June: There were to be speeches and recognitions and many, many soapy reminiscences, as well as a concert by the school band in which any old-timer who still had chops was urged to sit in. There would also be a sort of round-robin basketball game, in which all credentialed former Bulldogs—hey, remember that last eight-point season?—were invited to participate, cheered on by—uh oh!—cheerleaders of yesteryear. That evening, the individual classes would split off for their own private dinners and parties.

For whatever reason, the Class of '51 had never had a reunion of its own, and many of us hadn't seen each other for a long, long time. I knew that for most of my old classmates, it surely promised to be a very big day indeed. But in the early summer of 1990, my second marriage had, as I described it afterward, "blown up in my face as abruptly as a letter bomb," and ever since that dreadful cataclysm I had been wreathed in the miasma of a difficult and painful divorce. In the midst of so stygian a darkness, not even the beguiling fantasy of one last shot at roundball glory could dispel the gloom—not even with Ellie Chadwick cheering on the sidelines! The upcoming reunion was the last thing on my mind.

Then, on the first Saturday of May 1991, I dragged myself to a Kentucky Derby party in Lexington, where I met a beautiful Belgian classical pianist named Hilda and fell in love on the spot, and within two weeks we had decided that we'd marry the instant my divorce was final. As you might suppose, this prospect brightened my horizons amazingly. Suddenly, I was feelin' frisky! Go Bulldogs!

Hilda, who was still wrapping up a couple of courses in grad school at UK, couldn't make it, so I drove up to Maysville alone on the morning of the reunion, in the nifty new Dodge Dakota pickup I had just given myself as a tender little prenuptial wedding present. The town was busy, the sidewalks swarming with people, the way they used to be in the days before the coming of Wal-Mart and K-Mart and their attendant strip malls, when downtown Maysville was the Saturday shopping destination for the whole surrounding area of rural northeastern Kentucky and southern Ohio. I found a parking space just up the street from Kilgus's— remarkably, they were still in business—and set forth on foot for the MHS auditorium, where the festivities were already under way.

On Kilgus's Corner I spotted the first familiar face, that of a stocky, jowly little gent in a shiny green polyester suit and a necktie (although the day was already shaping up as a scorcher), who stood rooted there on the sidewalk like a fireplug as the pedestrian traffic surged about him. He was anxiously but furtively searching the faces of the passersby, as though he were looking for someone but didn't want to be noticed doing it. I knew immediately—those doleful brown eyes gave him away—that here was my long-ago hero and friend and rival, Dog. But just now he put me in mind of yet another canine personality, namely the bumbling old-time movie detective Bulldog Drummond. All that was wanted to complete the characterization was a bowler hat.

When Dog saw me approaching he quickly looked away, but then, tacitly acknowledging that he'd been recognized, he turned back to me and stuck out his hand in greeting.

"Hullo, Clammer," he said, forcing a smile. "How they hangin'?"

I allowed, as we shook hands, that they were hangin' pretty well, all things considered. Although it wasn't yet 11 AM, Dog's immediate aura was pungent with the redolence of what my long experience and highly refined olfactory sensibilities told me was blended whiskey, and not very good blended whiskey at that. His brow was beaded with sweat, and he was still glancing avidly at the faces in the passing parade—and I was pretty sure I knew who he was looking for. I asked him if he planned to play in the veteran Bulldogs' shoot-out that afternoon, and he answered, almost irritably, Nah, hell no, and then—same old Dog—asked if I had a cigarette on me. I apologized for the fact that I'd stopped using them years ago, and he said Yeah, he had quit a while back too, but for some reason he was really wanting one this morning. I laughed and said, Hey man, a guy's *gotta* smoke on Kilgus's Corner, it's the law! But Dog didn't seem to see the humor in that, so I said I'd catch him later, and set out again for the auditorium.

I crossed the street and paused in the shade of the marquee of the now-defunct Schine's Russell Theatre, to look back. Dog was still standing on the corner, scanning the crowded sidewalk, keeping a Bulldog Drummond eye out, I was sure, for the merest glimpse of Ellie Chadwick.

Inside the auditorium, the class of '87 or '86 or some other irrelevant year was doing its presentation, so I plunged into the large company of folks milling about outside. During the next hour, I reunited with untold numbers of old schoolmates: My great pal Ray Toncray was there with Shirley, his

wife of thirty-eight years, for whose favors Ray and I had con-
tended when she was still Shirley Collings, a sultry, smoky-
voiced teen temptress; and Jannie Batchelor who, as Bernice
Stonebreaker, is the Jezebel of "Great Moments in Sports,"
the story that leads off this book (Dog is in that one too, by
the way; he's one of those accursed Bobbys); and Denyse
and Joyce and Ann and June and my old sweetie Laura Lou,
and dear Lucia who failed so miserably to teach me how to
trip the light fantastic; and Freddie Hamm, who beat me
out for class salutatorian, the only academic honorific I was
ever in the running for; and Jerry and Gera and Billy the
Byrdman and Dody and Breezy and Dooner and Nancy
and Tubby; and Gerry Calvert, who was, along with Como
and the peerless Kenny Reeves, one of Maysville High's
three immortals; and Willie Gordon Ryan, to whom (prod-
uct placement alert!) *The Natural Man* is dedicated; and
Bob Z., that rarest of rare birds, a lovable lawyer; and most
piquant and soul-stirring of all, perhaps, my long-ago secret
squeeze Yvonne (let's call her), still strikingly handsome in
her mid-fifties, who had been my first genuine conquest
when I was barely seventeen and she was . . . careful now . . .
somewhat younger.

(Yvonne and I even managed to step away from the crowd
outside the auditorium long enough to reminisce, briefly,
about that all-too-brief occasion. "I'm afraid I wasn't really
very good at it," I admitted ruefully. "Well, no," Yvonne
acknowledged, "not very." And then she smiled and leaned

closer and added, just above a whisper, what are surely the most generous words any woman has ever said to me: "But didn't we have fun!")

I caught a couple of glimpses of Dog lurking about the fringes of the gathering, alone and, as the poet has it, palely loitering. I figured I probably knew the reason for his melancholy, because so far I hadn't seen the first sign of Ellie Chadwick. After a third sighting of the crestfallen Dog, I sought out my old friend Ann Crockett, who was a principal organizer of the reunion, and asked if she knew whether Ellie planned to come down to Maysville for the celebration. Ann said she'd talked to Ellie last night on the phone — first time in years, Ann said — and that she'd promised to be here in time for the basketball game, and even to join the renascent cheerleaders as — I'm extrapolating now — they'd be strutting their vintage stuff in one last, rousing turn on the sidelines, while doddering Bulldogs lumbered up and down the hardwood trying to catch up with the elusive ghosts of their lost youth.

"She's a little nervous about . . . you-know-who," Ann confided. "She's afraid he might try to . . . start something."

Don't worry, I assured her, Dog's a good guy; once he sees it's not working, he won't do anything to embarrass himself. But Ann said she was actually thinking more along the lines of his doing something that might embarrass Ellie — and also, she reminded me pointedly, it was not for nothing that they'd named him Bulldog.

While Ann and I were talking, the reconstituted MHS band struck up a rather lame "My Old Kentucky Home" (Guy Lumbago lives!) and everybody hobbled into the auditorium as docilely as ninth-graders on Assembly Day. Inside, the band labored through a few more numbers, after which the speeches resumed, with a vengeance; there were more class presentations (Class of '58, Class of '57, Class of '56), and interspersed with those were tributes—to Johnny Faris the legendary band director, to Miss Collins the legendary math teacher, to Miss Wallingford the legendary English teacher, and most especially to the legendary Coach Jones, who languished in a nursing home—and by the time the program got down to the Class of '51, the basketball debacle had long since begun next door in the gymnasium, and virtually the entire audience had decamped and moved on to that more alluring venue.

Which was fine with me, except that a couple of days ago someone on the organizing committee had called me in Lexington and asked me to deliver a few remarks as a part of our presentation. So I had composed an amusing but highly edifying little address rhapsodizing that long-ago first night on the town with Gene and Johnny, featuring Wild Bill's death-defying aerobatics atop the bridge—and now I was obliged to off-load my poetic reflections upon an audience of about six restive souls in a small, once-familiar auditorium that had suddenly turned into the Hollywood Bowl.

That ordeal concluded (to a smattering of applause that barely eclipsed the sound of one hand clapping), I hurried over to the old gymnasium, where I found that there were still a few dozen fans in the stands, and that the classes of '50 and '51 had combined forces, and were challenging the classes of '52 and '53 — call it the Geezers vs. the Gaffers — to a five-minute geriatric pickup game. The band was there too, cranking out a wheezy rendition of "The MHS Fight Song" ("It's a grand old school . . . And we follow the rule . . . And we fight for the gold and the white"). On the sidelines, far across the floor, was a gaggle of ladies in street clothes, flouncing and bouncing and capering and gamboling, chanting, "V-I-C-T-O-R-Y! Victory, Victory, Maysville High!" In their midst — be still, my heart! — was Ellie Chadwick, looking, at least to my forgiving old eyes, as fresh and blond and winsome and bountifully voluptuous as she had been forty years ago.

Way up in the upper-left-hand corner of the grandstand, I spotted a small, roundish figure, all alone, roosting up there in the rafters like a pigeon with shiny green polyester plumage.

I took a seat on the bench and waited for one of my Geezer teammates to crap out. It didn't take long: After the doughty relics had pounded up and down the floor for two or three minutes, I. Jay Weaver, panting like a pufferbelly — those Class of 1950 guys are getting up in years, poor devils — took himself out of the lineup for a breather with the score knotted at 4–4, and into the breach strode . . . Eddie the Intimidator!

Now, as Tall Eddie takes the floor in the vast gymnasium

of his imagination, a mighty roar arises, and Ellie Chadwick leads the multitudes—McClanafans all, their numbers magically swollen to the hundreds, the thousands, nay, the tens of thousands—in yet another full-throated cheer: "He's a wonder, he's a dream! He's the captain of our team! Yay, rah rah, EDDIE!" On the very first play, he soars like an eagle to block the great Gerry Calvert's lay-up, pull down the rebound, drive the floor, and put up a thirty-foot jumper! String music! "V-I-C-T-O-R-Y! Yay, rah rah, EDDIE!"

The reality, needless to say, was a little different: In that version, I distinguish myself only by getting bowled over by my old pal Ray Toncray—make that my former old pal—as he unleashes an up-yours jump shot in the final seconds that wins the game for the Gaffers, 8–6. When the buzzer sounds, concluding our allotted five minutes, I am ignominiously picking my elderly self up off the ancient and dangerously splintery hardwood. The band, meanwhile, has packed up and is already filing out of the stands, and the cheerleaders seem to have left the premises. Dog, apparently, has done likewise.

The Class of '51 banquet was to be held that evening at a venerable Maysville establishment called Caproni's, down in the West End on—believe it!—Rosemary Clooney Street. There would also be an after-party at the Ramada Inn, where I and most of my out-of-town classmates were staying, the flagship attraction of a profoundly unlovely new strip mall

up on the hill above town. So, my unaccustomed constitu-
tional in that hothouse of a gym having left me as damp as
a steamed clam, I repaired to the Ramada for a desperately
needed shower and some fresh clothes and, thus improved
and restored, a little before-dinner drink, in grateful celebration of the long-anticipated arrival of the cocktail hour.

I took my celebratory drink to the window of my second-
floor room, where I stood gazing out upon the Ramada's
asphalt parking lot and, beyond the rooftops of downtown
Maysville far below, a panoramic vista of northeastern
Kentucky farmland stretching off to the distant horizon,
rumpled as an unmade bed, with ridges and gullies and
hollers fanning out into infinity. It was a scenic prospect
that could have been duplicated from almost any eminent
vantage point in that part of the state, but—I realized with
a start as I stood there at the window, sipping my scotch
from a motel-issue plastic cup while the air conditioner blew
frigid zephyrs up my pants legs—I'd seen this particular view
before, under very different circumstances. For the Ramada
Inn stands exactly athwart what was once the ridge-runner
tobacco patch in which I'd labored through the dog days of
1949, performing mighty Sisyphean deeds with my magic
singing garden hoe.

And then I remembered something else: Forty-two sum-
mers ago, when I was plugging wearily along in that shade-
less, sweltering tobacco patch, I was regularly sustained in
my sufferings by the enduring fantasy that if and when I ever

got to the end of this everlasting goddamn row—or the next one, or the next after that—I'd find there a great, spreading shade tree, and beneath it would be, yes, Ellie Chadwick, clad not in one of her usual modest schoolgirl frocks but in Daisy Mae's unvarying wardrobe—that skimpy, tattered skirt! that off-the-shoulder blouse! (you remember, the yellow one, with the big dark polka dots the size of chocolate chip cookies!)—my very own personal Ellie Chadwick, recumbent in the deep, cool grass, fetching as a stand of buttercups, an Ellie Chadwick blow-up doll filled to bursting with the Divine McClanafflatus, awaiting me with open arms!

I raised my plastic cup of scotch in tribute to the vision, even as it faded into the ether and left me toasting the sun-blasted Ramada parking lot, vacant now except for my blue Dakota pickup.

When I arrived at Cap's, our party was in full swing in the private dining room; there was a long banquet table all laid out for dinner, and a cash bar open for business, with many of my classmates and their assorted spouses gathered round it, drinking and reminiscing in approximately equal measure, as though there were no tomorrows, only yesterdays. I picked up a drink at the bar and, true to my bent, intrepidly plunged headlong into the revelry.

Once again, Dog's was the first familiar face I encountered, and as before, he was in the crowd but not *of* it; he stood off to the side, a drink in one hand and a cigarette in the other, having a conversation of sorts with our old Bulldog teammate Willie Gordon Ryan. Dog's outer man had not been improved by the day's exertions, which had evidently required a considerable further infusion of blended whiskey. He still wore his wash-and-wear suit, but it had become rumpled and disheveled, in need of less wear and more wash; he'd unbuttoned his shirt collar and loosened his tie to receive the evening airs, and his five o'clock shadow was asserting itself on his jowls with seven o'clock authority; and although he stood more or less upright, he seemed to list, ever so slightly, just a degree or two off the perpendicular, now to the left, now to the right, like the pendulum of a clock that needed winding.

Willie Gordon, who was usually taciturn but seemed at the moment to be in an animated conversational mode, was apparently trying to recreate a moment in some historic Bulldog game, shooting free throws with an invisible basketball, putting up imaginary shots in the old style—two-handed, from between the knees—that Coach Jones had insisted on. But Dog was so obviously not giving Willie Gordon's story his full attention that after a minute or two Willie Gordon gave it up, shrugged elaborately, and drifted off to freshen his refreshment. Dog barely noticed; his bleary but still discerning eye was drawn to the far corner of the room, beyond the banquet table, where there was a smaller table at which were assembled some half a dozen ladies—girls, if you please—Denyse and Joyce and Lucia and two or three others, Ellie Chadwick prominent among them. They were in deep confab over their drinks, taking sweet girlish counsel together, exactly as they used to do when they were talking about boys in their favorite booth at Kilgus's, back when the world was young. Judging from the wary sidelong glances which several of them—though never Ellie—darted now and then in Dog's direction, he was apparently the subject of their current speculations. Ellie herself steadfastly looked the other way, but, girls being girls, it was a pretty good bet that by now they'd brought her up to speed on the long history (as they understood it) of the grand romance in which she figured so prominently.

Ann Crockett, who happened to be standing next to me in the crowd around the bar, and who was observing this tableau as intently as I was, sighed and mused, almost to herself, "Poor fellow, he's still wild about her, isn't he?" I said it looked to me like she had that about right, but that it didn't surprise me much, because so was I. "Oh, well," said Ann, with a smile and an empathetic wave of her hand that was intended to include every male in the room, "aren't you all?"

I didn't even need to concede the point, for there before me, beckoning like a shimmering beacon in the dark night of the soul, was Ellie's finely wrought profile, quite as exquisite as it had been that first morning forty-three years ago in Miss Wallingford's tenth-grade English class. As I approached her table she turned her lovely countenance full upon me—the force of it struck me like a cannonball smack to the brisket, yet somehow I managed not to stagger—and rose immediately to give me a hug, which was heartening, inasmuch as the very fact that she recognized me at all seemed, momentarily, to suggest that I was as unchanged by the years as she was—until I reminded myself that (1) she had presumably witnessed my heroics in the basketball game a few hours earlier, and (2), like everyone else in the room, I was wearing, pinned to my lapel, a name tag the size of a lawyer's shingle. Still, I was happy to be greeted so warmly by so beautiful a woman, and made doubly happy by her promise, before I moved along to say hello to someone at the next table, that we'd surely find a chance to talk later in the evening.

At dinner, I found myself seated opposite Ellie—imagine Scarlett Johansson as she'll be, if she's a very lucky girl, at fifty-eight or fifty-nine—a circumstance so distracting that it has completely erased my recollection of who my neighbors at the table were, or of who Ellie's neighbors were, or of what was eaten, drunk, or said throughout that epic rubber-chicken repast—except for one brief but ineradicable memory which, like those painful televised home videos of people making asses of themselves, is even now in rerun on the small screen of my memory. Here's how it goes:

After our devout classmate the Very Rev. Lester G. Pullet, pastor of the East End Four Square Pentecostal Little Brown

Kirk o' the Wildwood, has unburdened himself of pieties beyond number by way of saying grace (while those of us who recall the obnoxiously priapic Les Pullit of his formative years suppress the impulse to snort and snigger), the Class of '51 coughs and clears its collective throat, seats itself, takes up its knives and forks, and is just preparing to tuck into its rubber chicken, when I hear, off to my left, the tink-tink-tink of a fork against a water glass. Dog has risen unsteadily to his feet, as if to propose a toast, or—heaven forefend, considering his condition—to make a speech. His eyes are rheumy and out of focus, and he has donned his old beseeching-mendicant mask, which must've served him well in the snack food sales game back in the day but is now in a state of slow meltdown, like a beagle morphing into a basset hound. Everybody in the room pretty much knows what's coming, and braces for it.

Which brings us to a moment I've long dreaded—for I had hoped, when I undertook to tell this story, that all the principal characters in it (with the possible exception of myself and Wild Bill Dugan) would emerge with their dignity essentially intact. But here's this pudgy, unprepossessing sixty-year-old inebriate in rumpled polyester, determined against all odds to fulfill a fantasy he's entertained for forty years, ready and even eager to make a spectacle of himself before an audience of the oldest and most admiring friends he'll ever have, the last people on earth who still remember him as the very best he'll ever be, the last of all those cheering multitudes in the stands at the old Armory gym in Louisville in 1947 who still remember how he and Como trotted out to center court in the golden glow of the Armory spotlight, side by side in their sleek white-and-gold sateen Bulldog warm-up jackets, to claim the first two All–Sweet Sixteen trophies ever taken home by a pair of eighth-graders.

(I was there too, I'll remind you, another eighth-grader way up in the Armory stands somewhere, that plump little apostate Polar Bear benchwarmer who would've given several testicles—preferably other people's—for one of those Bulldog jackets.)

Dog's little speech that night at Cap's—it only lasted a couple of minutes—was eloquent, even though the miasma of blended whiskey had so befuddled his mind and befuck-led his articulation that much of what he said was imme-diately lost to history, and even though what remained was basically just an expression of his lifelong amber . . . adner . . . his ad-mi-*ray*-shun for . . . a shertain shpecial pershon (across the table, Ellie looked stricken), eloquent nonethe-less for all it tried to say about love and loss and longing, about all the travails to which the human heart tremulously subjects itself.

As Dog muddled on, some at the banquet table laughed uneasily, some were aghast, a few (I'd like to think I was among them) winced, and looked pained. Ellie blushed, then paled, and tears welled briefly in her fine blue eyes—

though whether they were tears of chagrin or embarrassment or even sympathy, I could not have said. Dog, meanwhile, after a sort of tipsy little wrestling match with himself while he fumbled for something inside his coat, unfurled before us, as triumphantly as though it were the Magna Carta or the Declaration of Independence or at least the Desiderata, a tiny six-by-six rice-paper scroll, upon which the entire (surviving) Class of '51 beheld at last the chimerical Treasure of the Orient, a delicate little pastel watercolor rendition of the same Skool Daze photo of Ellie Chadwick that I too had revered so long ago. A certifiable masterpiece; in my youth I would've sacrificed any number of other people's testicles for it.

Throughout Dog's interminable two-minute dumb show, I entertained a competing fantasy: Any second now I just might leap to my feet and tink-tink-tink Dog into submission and seize control of this whole unseemly situation! Tall Eddie Clammerham into the breach! To spare Ellie further indignities, I would rise up and take the floor myself!

But of course once I had the floor I'd be needing something to say while I held it, so maybe I'd just reiterate those stirring but little-noted remarks I had addressed to the empty auditorium earlier that same afternoon, featuring my anecdote about Wild Bill and the bridge. Yes! If Tall Eddie's prowess on the hardwood has fallen a tad short of the expectations of those invisible legions of McClanafans worldwide—fear not, dear hearts, his wit and art and charm will save the day! Yay, rah rah, Eddie!

While Dog and I were simultaneously indulging our mutually exclusive delusions, Ellie regained her composure. Her gaze was now as grave and dignified and immutable as a marble statue of Miss Wallingford—and to Dog, seeing her through a diaphanous veil of blended whiskey, she must've seemed, suddenly, just about as unobtainable. The effect, I guess, was sobering, for whatever lugubrious nonsense Dog happened, just then, to be mouthing trailed off into an awkward silence. Without another word, he pocketed the little scroll, dropped heavily into his chair, and took refuge behind his chicken cacciatore. So Tall Eddie's intervention wouldn't be required after all. My work here was done.

Well, actually, not quite. For one thing, there was Caproni's famous rubber-chicken cacciatore to be confronted, and dealt with. For another, there was Ellie Chadwick, a scant four feet away, to be distracted by.

As I've already confessed, I have no recollection at all of who Ellie's and my dinner companions might have been, although we both assiduously carried on a conversation with all of them throughout the banquet, and hardly spoke a word to one another. Dog was seated down-table to my left, out of my line of sight, and I couldn't help noticing that while the rest of us regaled ourselves, Ellie kept glancing warily in his direction, as though he might suddenly dart under the table and reappear beside her chair, sitting up, panting, begging for scraps.

And that unfortunate image, forbearing reader, will have to be the last we'll see of Dog in these pages. But I hate to leave him like that, diminished almost to insignificance by my own metaphor, when in fact I can't help thinking that there was actually something rather fine and noble in his long, undeviating passion. That forty years of quixotic wandering in the wilderness should, in the end, go unrewarded was pretty much a foregone conclusion—failure being a precondition of quixotic endeavors, as windmills everywhere can attest—but at least it needn't go unremarked. So whatever else this story proves to be, consider it a tribute to Dog's devotion and perseverance and even—battered though it must have been, at that point—to his pride. Of *course* he wouldn't have wanted to waddle his portly, aging person onto the floor this afternoon for the old-timers' game, knowing Ellie would be on the sidelines; after all, the last time he'd played before her, he weighed 150 compact pounds, and was a certified All-State demigod!

Yet leave him we must, for in a matter of moments, while everyone else's attention is diverted by the arrival of dessert, Ellie will lean across the table, her face so close to mine that I can almost count her eyelashes, and murmur, in a voice as soft as a maiden's blush, with one more wary blue-eyed sidelong glance in the direction of the fallen demigod, "Eddie, would you mind taking me up to the Country Club?"

Regrettably, this was not destined to be that long-awaited occasion when Ellie would spirit me off to some exotic clime to take advantage of me and, if all went well, use me horribly. Rather, the situation was just that he—she meant Dog—was really making her uneasy, and since her older brother Tom was up on the hill above town at the Maysville Country Club, where the Class of '48 was having its own reunion party, she thought maybe I wouldn't mind . . .

Mind? Hadn't I waited forty years to bird-dog that canine interloper? To borrow the rousing call to arms of Mistopher Snuffy Smif, Li'l Abner's fellow cartoon hillbilly, "Time's a-wastin'!"

But it went without saying that we mustn't make our move until the moment was precisely right—which happened, fortuitously, just a few minutes later, when Dog left the table and staggered off in the general direction of the Gents. Tipping Ellie a surreptitious wink, I excused myself as though I were hastening to the same destination—and slipped, instead, out the front door, and within seconds Ellie was at my side in the Dakota, and we were scratchin' off in Cap's parking lot.

There's a short way and a long way to get to the Maysville Country Club from Caproni's, and you may be sure I took the latter—down West Second to the end of town, three miles up the hill to Jersey Ridge Road, then another five or six miles across Jersey Ridge to the Club. After executing that dashing teenage scratch-off, I cleverly downshifted into geezer slo-go, and what could have been a ten-minute drive became a half-hour luxury cruise of backstreets and back roads, during which Ellie and I, historically as incommunicative as a pair of oysters on a blind date, chattered like magpies at a . . . okay, at a magpie class reunion. After all, we had, between us, eight decades of sheer, unadulterated autobiography to account for—and I don't do unadulterated autobiography myself, so the time allotted me for autobiographical purposes tends to expand from within, like a hot air balloon. (The Divine McClanafflatus never sleeps!) Moreover, although by unspoken mutual agreement Ellie and I never once mentioned Dog, we quickly found that we had a vast amount to say about all the other lapsed acquaintances we'd renewed that day, and about how well—or ill—the last forty years had served our erstwhile schoolmates. We couldn't have squoze all that prattle into those ten miles if I'd been driving a horse and buggy.

Accordingly, as we clippetty-clopped along Jersey Ridge Road in our air-conditioned 200-horse Dodge powerbuggy, it briefly crossed my calculating mind to cop a quick left on Rosemont Lane and continue our conversation out on Rosemont Point, once the premier park-and-spark spot of the known world, an eminence that overlooks the lights of Maysville, the bridge, and the great, sweeping north bend of the broad Ohio, the very spot where the captivating Yvonne, that lucky girl, had had her way with me under a buttermilk sky in 1949, in the incommodious backseat of my mom's two-door Chevy sedan. Rosemont Point! Who knows? Tonight, right out there on Rosemont Point, Ellie Chadwick just might get lucky too!

But then there was the distinct possibility—make that the overwhelming likelihood—that Ellie would have, in 1991, even less enthusiasm for a second date with me than she'd had in 1948, as well as the looming certainty that Hilda, my lovely trophy-bride-to-be, would have none at all, and would surely be inclined to leave my unworthy nether person at the altar in the bargain. Then too, Rosemont Lane had somehow become (according to the classy black-and-gilt sign that arced above the entrance, between stone gateposts topped by rampant, miniature cast-iron stallions) "Rosemont Point Estates, An Arabian Horse Community." I breathed a small sigh of regret (with just a whisper of relief), and drove on.

At the Country Club, all the classes of the 1940s, their numbers so depleted by the years (poor devils) that they couldn't muster quorums of their own, had combined for their reunion, and had engaged Woody Wood (Class of '46) and His Swinging Woodpeckers for their after-dinner dancing pleasure. (Woodson T. Wood, Esq., Attorney at Law, had been the trombone virtuoso of the MHS Marching Band, and had never quite recovered from it.) Already, by the time Ellie and I arrived, the Woodpeckers were on the bandstand, swingin' pretty lively, and several sprightly duos of doughty old parties were fox-trotting about the dance floor as though they were eighth-graders again, back at Mrs. Brown's School of the Dance.

We joined Ellie's brother Tom and his pals at the Class of '48 table, and were soon rewarded by the realization that, in this company, we were the eighth-graders! From the perspective of your average sexagenarian, it seemed, persons in their late fifties are in the bloom of youth and simultaneously at the very cusp of senescence—temporarily immortal, so to speak—capable of absorbing prodigious quantities of alcohol as long as it comes mixed with veiled warnings of impending decrepitude—which is to say that everybody wanted to buy us drinks and tell us about their hip replacements.

(Ten years later, after I'd had my own hip replacement, I understood a little better where they were coming from.)

When we'd enjoyed a sufficiency (not to say a surfeit) of these attentions, I actually managed to lure Ellie onto the dance floor, hoping to resume our conversation and also to demonstrate that—having unlearned the box-step one night in 1966 under the combined influence of Owsley acid, the Grateful Dead, and the strobe lights of the Fillmore Auditorium—I was no longer the Frankenstinian toe-stomper she had known and endured. But talking-while-dancing was still beyond my powers, especially with Woody and the boys blasting away as though there were seventy-six trombones on the bandstand; so after we'd danced a couple of numbers, I ventured the suggestion that we sneak outside where we could carry on our conversation unimpeded by all these noisy old pooperoos.

The upshot of this cunning bit of strategy was that Ellie and I spent one last deliciously innocent hour sitting in my pickup in the country club parking lot, talking like teapots. For my part, I wanted her to know that she'd been my beau ideal ever since I used to write her name all over my school-books in Miss Wallingford's English class (I told her about the handful of caterpillars, but didn't mention that they were in flagrante delicto), and how unworthy I had felt when she invited me to escort her to the Sadie Hawkins Dance, how utterly inadequate to that monumental endeavor I had believed—and subsequently proved—myself to be. But I had been out of my depth, I hastened to explain, pleading my case; I was just a hapless Bracken County clod, lately and precipitately plucked from his natural churlish element (presumably a Bracken County pigpen) and plunged up to his churlish earlobes in *le grand monde de Maysville*, with no idea under Heaven how to conduct himself in polite society.

Ellie giggled charmingly at my characterization of my juvenile self, and said that personally she had always con-sidered me a Very Nice Sort of Boy (which was generous of her, although, on balance, I believe I'd have preferred being remembered as a lout), and that, at the time, she'd probably been almost as disoriented as I was, her family having moved to Maysville in 1947, only a year before I got there myself. (This was news to me; I guess I'd always assumed she had sprung forth full-blown right there on the banks of the Ohio, like Venus on the Half-Shell.) Moreover, the Chadwicks were from Louisville, meaning that if my move from Brooksville had been like hopping from a frog pond into Esther Williams's private pool, then Ellie's move from Louisville would've been (to pour on the aquatic imagery beyond all human capacity to absorb it) like netting a mermaid in the South Pacific and depositing her in a goldfish bowl.

Otherwise, we pretty much steered clear of the historio-autobiographical imperative, and applied ourselves instead to telling each other, rather excitedly, about recent developments in our vastly separate worlds—breaking news, as it were.

My breathless, this-just-in story was, of course, all about the bolt-from-the-blue advent of Hilda in what had been—and what remains even now, more than fifteen years after she brought the light that saw me through it—the gloomiest passage of my life. And I had pictures! So there I was, sitting beside one of the two most beautiful women I'd ever known, proudly showing her, by the Dakota's feeble dome light, photos of the other one! Moments when you'd like to live forever! Anyhow, it was a pretty good story, and as (knowing me) you might suppose, it took me a while to tell it to my satisfaction. But Ellie patiently heard me out and, once again, she followed it up with a pretty good story of her own:

Back home in Massachusetts, she said, she had been involved for some time in an effort (which, by the way, would ultimately prove successful) to save a famous New England landmark of American literature from some enlightened developer who wanted to turn it into an amusement park. So a few weeks ago, her preservationist group had held a garden party fund-raiser (I envisioned a dappled hilltop meadow with ancient stone walls and gnarly old apple trees and lots of ladies in white frocks and picture hats; I'm very big on picture hats), and my then-current rising political hero, the handsome, nationally ambitious young governor of Arkansas—who regularly vacationed at nearby Martha's Vineyard, and whose eye for the ladies was already acquiring a certain notoriety—had been a celebrity presence at the occasion. And Ellie had met him! In person!

So how did you like him? I inquired eagerly.

"We-e-ell," she answered, after a long moment of moderate Republican hesitation, "I'm not too sure about his politics. But . . . he complimented my hat!"

Suddenly I saw it all exactly as the young future president of the United States himself must have seen it: Above him the blue, blue Massachusetts sky flocked with snow-white apple blossoms, before him the ravishing, going-on-sixty divorcée in her billowing white Marilyn Monroe frock, her incandescent blue-eyed smile picture-perfect in the perfect circle of the picture hat—and the courtly future president finds himself, for perhaps the first time in his eventful young life, at a loss for words. Flummoxed, he gulps and grins and bites his lower lip in that ingratiating Li'l Abner way of his and stammers, "Ma'am, Ah . . . Ah sho'ly do admire yo' hat!"

"Ellie, my dear," I said, biting my own lip to suppress an insinuating chuckle, "I hate to break this to you, but I don't think it was really your hat that he was looking at."

I had lowered the Dakota's windows to catch the evening breeze, and now from inside the clubhouse we heard, signaling the party's end, the distant strains of "Good Night, Sweetheart"—and considering that the hour was late and Woody and the Woodpeckers were, to a man, well into both their cups and their sixties, "strains" was definitely the applicable word. In any case, the time had come for Ellie and me to say our own good nights, and our good-byes as well, since she was to spend the night with her brother and his family in Cincinnati, and then to catch an early plane for Boston in the morning. As a parting tribute, I gave her a copy of one of my books, and even condescended, with becoming authorial modesty, to sign it for her—"For Ellie with love, xoxo, Eddie"—thereby presenting those frolicsome caterpillars with one last unseemly turn upon the stage. But Ellie didn't notice what they were up to. She just thanked me by way of a warm hug and a sweet little peck on the cheek, we said good-bye again, and she was gone.

Back at the Ramada, I found that the Class of '51 after-party was basically over too. Willie Gordon Ryan and a couple of other guys were sitting outside by the pool, enjoying a nightcap and taking the midnight air. They offered me a drink, which of course I took, and joshed me a bit about sneaking off with Ellie, which of course I denied—but not very convincingly, I'm afraid, because I couldn't stop grinning.

Dog, Willie Gordon said, had failed to reappear from Cap's men's room for quite a while, until finally someone discovered him passed out in one of the stalls and called his nephew (Vernon, Class of '63), who'd had to leave his own class party to come and haul his uncle away, peevishly vowing all the while to deliver the delightful old soak to the Lexington airport first thing tomorrow morning and pour him onto a plane bound for Florida and be done with him.

It was time to call it a day. I polished off my nightcap, said so long to my old pals, and went up to my room—where the first thing I did, rest assured, was fix myself another nightcap. Then I doused the light and took my drink to the window, as before, opened the curtains, and stood there for a long time, looking out beyond the dark brow of the hill upon the lights of Maysville far below, pondering all the momentous moments that had transpired during that momentous day . . . and all the ones that hadn't.

In the latter category were my inspiring oration in the auditorium, my game-winning last-second jump shot in the ball game, and my four-decades-late tryst with Ellie on Rosemont Point; in the former were two whispered confidences— "But didn't we have fun!" and "Eddie, would you mind taking me up to the Country Club?"—and a soft, almost evanescent kiss on the cheek whose imprint lingered like a memory.

And in an empty gym somewhere down there in the hometown of my heart, a phantom band played on—"We're from ol' Kentuck . . . And we're full of pluck . . . Maysville's always right!"—and phantom cheerleaders were still chanting, "He's a wonder, he's a dream! He's the captain of our team!"

HOW'S THAT AGAIN?

LEXINGTON, April 2003—Recently (say for about the last decade, or roughly eighty percent of our married life), the Madam has been on my case about having my hearing tested—usually just after I've been on hers about her unfortunate habit of mumbling. Heedless to my admonishments, she just mumbles on and on; when it comes to listening to reason, the woman is as deaf as a hammer.

But one fine day last fall, I had an experience that gave me pause.

It started that morning, when the UPS brownie (get it? brownie?) delivered, to my delight, the swank new $189.95

goatsuede jacket I'd ordered from the Rugged Fogy o' the Old West catalog. The fit was just right, and for a while I strutted about the house, quite pleased with my new goat-suede Outer Man, imagining I favored that TV lawyer, Gerry Spence, with his fringed buckskins and flowing white locks—until I caught a glimpse of myself in a mirror, and recognized not Gerry Spence but Gabby Hayes. Eventually, the Madam mumbled—better make that "muttered grimly"—that she'd seen enough nonproductive preening, and sent me off to run some errands.

So I'm tooling about town on this nice autumn afternoon in my little Kentucky Wildcat Blue '96 Toyota RAV4—for reasons I'll explain momentarily, his name is Cleave—running my errands and tolerantly allowing the odious Rush Limbaugh to shout at me at the top of his odious lungs (I've noticed lately that if I don't turn the volume up, Rush has a tendency to mumble), when it occurred to me that Cleave's own Outer Vehicle was looking pretty scruffy, and needed attention. Would Gerry Spence gad about in muddy rolling stock? Time to spruce up! Giddyap, Cleave!

Now, while we're toddling out Winchester Road to the car wash, let me seize the opportunity to make it clear that I don't generally hold much for the sentimentalizing or anthropomorphizing of vehicles, no matter how endearingly or infuriatingly sentient they sometimes seem. The practice does have literary antecedents—Gurney Norman's Urge, Ken Kesey's Furthur, my own late VW microbus, the

McClanavan, and her asthmatic old traveling companion, Moldy Dick—but in the main, assigning one's motorized conveyance an affectionate nickname—"Ole Bessie," or "Peaches," or "Buckfuddy"—is a risky proposition at best, considering that, like Shakespeare's thankless child with the serpent's tooth, sooner or later the beast will surely turn on you, or fail you in some time of need or crisis, and reduce you to kicking its tires in rage and frustration—no way to treat a member of the family.

Anyhow, at the time of the adventure from which we're presently digressing, Cleave had no nickname at all, despite the fact that he'd been my good and faithful servant for the past six years, and had just last summer borne me all the way to Oregon and back without a whimper. Nonetheless, although it was my devout hope that my RAV4 and I held lifetime warranties on each other, Cleave didn't acquire a name of his own until, sadly, the recent ice storm that was the crashing grand finale of this dismal winter, when a tree fell on him and clove his little blue noggin right down the middle. Hence, Cleave.

As of this writing, Cleave's on life support at the body shop, and it's a tossup whether he's going to make it or be . . . totalled. Stay tuned on that. Meanwhile, back to our story:

At the new Winchester Road automated drive-thru car wash, I'm discovering that the word "automated" is more nuanced than I'd supposed, and the term "drive-thru" a downright misnomer. For starters, the automated cashier rejects my money—treats me like a goddamn counterfeiter, if you want to know. But then what—or who—turns up but, of all things, a human being!

There's an attendant, it seems, a pleasant young man who takes my dough and gives me change and directs me to pull forward into a sort of bay, where he personally applies a soothing balm of soapy prewash to my RAV4's grubby exterior, while I resume my argument with Rush. The prepping accomplished, the pleasant young man motions for me to ease my front wheels onto the trolley-track affair which is to guide me into the maelstrom of great whirling, swirling brushes and cascading waters just ahead.

And right there is where the drive-thru ends and the drag-thru begins.

Suddenly, with a heavy metallic clank, some unseen mechanism reaches up from the hellish car wash under-world and grabs Cleave-to-be by the short hairs and uncer-emoniously yanks us toward the roaring car wash Niagara even as I realize that the pleasant young man is now to my immediate left at the driver's-side window gesturing excit-edly and mouthing what I interpret as "Put your foot on the brake and put the car in gear!" which seems passing strange because that's what I'm already doing anyhow, but the pleas-ant young man keeps on gesturing and shouting until finally I roll the window down halfway (for the purpose of telling him to stop mumbling, fer crissakes) and hear instead "Take your foot off the brake and take the car out of gear!" (as any competent audiologist can tell you, "put" and "take" sound remarkably alike under certain atmospheric conditions), but before I can sort out and obey these apparently contradictory instructions the car lurches forward—"lurch" is going to be the operative word from here on—and I see to my horror that rushing toward me is this great hideous spongy pink alien thing with long flabby tentacles slapping at my fenders, my hood, my windshield, and now these vile slimy pink tendrils are actually *inside* the car, flippetty-flappetty-flopping through the still half-open window, invading my personal space and flinging nasty car wash juices all over me and my glasses and my nice upholstery and my new goatsuede jacket, and I'm frantically trying to poke them back out with one hand while fumbling for the electric window button with the other, but the more tentacles I push out the more come flopping in behind them, the car lurches again, lurch lurch lurch, I still have my foot on the brake and the car is still in gear but I'm far too busy to deal with that right now, my finger finds the button and the window goes up and closes on several limp flabby sopping tentacles, I lower it to fling them out whereupon the terrible pink alien instantly expels a jet of hot soapy venom that strikes me right between the eyes, Rush Limbaugh calls me a contemptible limp-wristed liberal and chortles insanely, lurch lurch, I finally get the last tentacle out and the window rolled up and lunge for the gearshift to yank it out of drive but in my haste almost succeed in slamming it into reverse instead, Cleave gnashes his metallic teeth alarmingly, together Cleave and I slip the ardent embrace of the rapacious extraterrestial rotating giant pink squid and with Rush fulminating volcanically about milksop liberals we lurch lurch lurch into the drying phase so that now we are buffeted by roaring tornadic blasts of hot air both without and within, I go for the volume knob and—imagining that I have Rush by his odious nose—twist it viciously leftward, and then . . .

And then it is as though a brief but terrible storm has passed, Rush abruptly hushes his odious mouth, and the dark car wash grotto where lurks the loathsome pink Shelob is somehow behind us, and Cleave and I are outside on the tarmac in the sunny afternoon, and the pleasant young man is tap-tap-tapping at my window.

After a quick glance at the rearview mirror to make sure the monster hasn't followed us out, I roll the window down.

"Next time, sir," the pleasant young man advises me, "put the car *out* of gear and—"

"Right!" I assure him brightly, tapping the accelerator in my eagerness to be elsewhere, *any* goddamn elsewhere, ASAP. "Absolutely, yes indeed, you bet!"

"—and take your foot *off* the—"

But Cleave and I are already making tracks, beating it, skedaddling for the barn. Giddyap, Cleave!

At home, when I breathlessly recount my ordeal to the Madam, she is utterly unsympathetic, and blames the whole thing on me—*me*, of all people!—for being such a horse's ass on the subject of hearing aids. (She doesn't actually say "horse's ass," of course, but I daresay we horse's asses can read between the lines as well as the next fellow.) Undaunted, I stick to my principles. No dice, I snort disdainfully, I hate those ugly little plastic wads that make a person look like he's parked his chewing gum in his ear! I'll get a hearing aid, I tell her, when they make a big red one! That's the ticket, designer hearing aids! Why the hell not? They make designer eyeglasses, don't they? I demand a hearing aid shaped like a pig's ear!

But the Madam (who is a Central European, and therefore not as advanced as we are) has heard all this before, and she is not impressed by my philosophy.

"Sweethearrrt," she coos, as I stalk off to lick my wounds and brush the water spots off my goatsuede jacket, "you are sotch a dummy sometimes."

And at this convenient impasse, our story ends—except that I promised an update on Cleave's condition, after that treacherous Ent (a goddamn water maple, wouldn't you know?) parted his hair and tried to make a dune buggy of him. Well, all of you who have joined me in praying for his recovery will be happy to learn that a few minutes ago Dr. Panelbeater called from the body shop to tell me it looks like Cleave is gonna be . . . okay!

At least I think that's what he said. The way some people mumble nowadays, there's just no telling.

THE IMP OF WRITING: ARS POETICA

When I was invited a while back to do a reading of my work for a group of student writers at a local college, the sponsor asked me to introduce my reading by briefly remarking on "the importance of writing." I made a note to myself—"imp. of wrtg."—on the appropriate date on my calendar, and promptly forgot all about it until, on the very eve of my scheduled appearance, I finally confronted the advisability of having something in mind to say before I actually came right out and said it. So I was mulling over the possibilities, none of which seemed very promising, when I happened to glance at my calendar and . . . there it was! The Imp of Writing! I could blame it all on the Imp of Writing! That scurrilous story in *Playboy* about my irrepressibly salty friend Little Enis, that salacious novel with all those gamy jokes . . . hey, the Imp of Writing made me do it!

For me, writing is a painstaking, intricately complex process that I can best liken to an altogether different art form, one about which, frankly, I know virtually nothing at all: composing music. I won't pretend that I've written any symphonies, but I do hope that every word I write—indeed, every single syllable—is a note in a little song, disguised as prose, that hums along inside my reader's head just below the level of consciousness. Like any aspiring Tin Pan Alley tunesmith, I use the devices of poetry—rhythm and assonance and alliteration, the internal cadences, the way the words play off against each other—to try to make my stories sing. But unlike, say, Rodgers & Hart, I bear sole responsibility for both the lyrics and the melody, and in my stories the language sometimes almost seems to drive the narrative, rather than the other way around, just as the melody of a song will sometimes shape the lyrics.

Or, to try another analogy on for size, writing is like performing brain surgery on yourself; you definitely don't want to do a rush job with it. The kind of prose I write requires a certain amount of precision, a good deal of coaxing, and vast quantities of patience, because it sometimes seems to take forever. Appearances to the contrary notwithstanding, it don't come easy, folks. But it's all just a slightly hyper attempt to capture your attention—"Look, Ma, no hands!"—in the hope that I can entertain you and amuse you and, with luck, touch your heart, and maybe even perform a little brain surgery on you when you're not looking.

"Write what you know," the ancient truism instructs us. How, pray tell, could you do otherwise? "What you know" is whatever's in your head, a seething, bubbling alchemical brew of your personal history and experience and genetics and various belief systems—and that most volatile of ingredients, your own mad, ungovernable imagination. So if your head is full of knights and dragons and fair ladies, that's what you'll write, regardless of whether or not you ever met a dragon socially. Poets and pornographers have at least this much in common: Their heads are full of what they write. Writing, as we used to put it back in the sixties, is an adventure in inner space; it will help you discover who you are, and what the world is. How do I know what I think, the saying goes, until I read what I've written? Writing will make you a better reader, a better thinker, and a better person.

The Imp of Writing has been sitting on my shoulder for some sixty years now, like an albatross, an organ grinder's monkey, a little bird with secrets to whisper, a tiny demon with a pitchfork, an angel with a halo. The Imp of the Perverse. The Muse. May you be so blessed.